LiVER COOKiES

Also by Dian Curtis Regan:

The Kissing Contest

Dian Curtis Regan

AN
APPLE
PAPERBACK

SCHOLASTIC INC.
New York Toronto London Auckland Sydney

ISBN 0-590-44337-2

Copyright © 1991 by Dian Curtis Regan. All rights reserved. Published by Scholastic Inc., 730 Broadway, New York, NY 10003. APPLE PAPERBACKS is a registered trademark of Scholastic Inc.

12 11 10 9 8 7 6 5 4 3 2 1   1 2 3 4 5 6/9

Printed in the U.S.A.   28

First Scholastic printing, May 1991

For Karen, Beth, and Gary Tripmacher

LIVER
COOKIES

1

"**E**n-tre-pre-neur. En-tre-pre-neur."

Holly Mann's oversized snow boots ker-plopped each syllable onto the steep cement steps rising to her front door. She didn't want to forget the word Beth Tipton had called her. *How dare she call me a name — even though she is my best friend.*

Holly unlocked the door, dumped her book bag, and grabbed the dictionary. Pulling a wool cap off her auburn hair, she picked up the phone, hitting the button that direct-dialed her dad's office.

Paging through the dictionary, Holly sounded out syllables until she found the word: "Entre-preneur," she read out loud. "One who organizes a business for profit."

Holly groaned as she tossed aside the dictionary and wiggled out of her heavy jacket, juggling the phone at her ear. "Sometimes I wish I knew what Beth was talking about without having to pretend."

1

"Pretend what?" came her dad's warm voice on the other end of the line. Holly ignored his question. "I'm home."

"You're a half hour late. What's wrong?"

"Sixth-graders had to stay after school to finish watching a health film," Holly explained, wishing her dad would ease up a little on his rules. "When Mrs. Molesworth showed the film this morning, the power went off halfway through because of the snowstorm."

Holly knew none of her friends back home in Los Angeles would ever believe it snowed here the second week of school. Alaska was a long way from California. It was a long way from her old friends, too.

And her mom.

Muffled voices came over the phone. Her dad must have covered the speaker with one hand to talk to his secretary. Holly thought it sounded like the speaker voice at the drive-up window at Eskimo Burgers.

Dad came back on the line. "Gotta go, Hol. We're pretaping an interview with the mayor for the five o'clock news."

"I'll be next door at Beth's. We have to invent a business as a project for Social Studies." Holly's brain instantly made the connection between the word Beth had called her and their project.

"What about — ?"

"Dinner will be ready when you get home." Her

dad had traumas whenever he suspected it was his turn to fix dinner.

"Mmmm," he answered, sounding like a lonely Alaskan moose. "I don't know where you got your talent for cooking, Holly Marie. It wasn't from me, and it *definitely* wasn't from your mother."

Holly hung up on his good-bye. Her stomach tightened whenever he mentioned Mom. And nine months in Ketchikan hadn't lessened the intensity of her reaction.

Keeping one eye on the clock, Holly hurried to the kitchen to collect a jar of homemade pasta sauce from the refrigerator. She grabbed two carrot sticks to munch, then returned to the living room, not wanting to leave for Beth's until she watched her mom's latest commercial on television.

"Ringgggggg!"

Holly pushed the speaker button on the phone so she could talk while pulling on her jacket. "Hello?" She halfway hoped it was Gary, Beth's little brother. But he'd never called before, so why should she hope?

"Holly, where *are* you?" Beth's voice was scolding. "I've already boiled the pasta, and I'm at a total standstill until you get here with the sauce."

"Be there in" — the alarm on Holly's watch beeped — "sixty seconds." She shut off the speaker phone and watch alarm — set so she wouldn't miss the commercial. Her mom always mailed schedules of the times she'd be appearing on national television.

The screen flickered, brightened, then Jacqueline Mann was there. Her auburn hair was pulled to one side. Vivid green eye shadow accented the same green eyes she shared with her daughter. A slinky gold dress bared one shoulder.

"Light and kicky," she was saying as she sprayed perfume toward the camera. "Yet becomes serious and mysterious when *you* want to be serious and mysterious."

On the word *mysterious*, Mom puckered her painted lips and winked her heavily mascara'd lashes for the camera.

Holly fell to her knees in front of the television, transfixed as a strange man in a tuxedo swung her mother around waltzlike, then carried her away through a misty cloud. All the while he gazed at her as if she'd just told him he'd been elected King of the World.

Falling onto her side, Holly grabbed her throat, pretending to gag to death. "Mo-om!" She made a face at the TV screen, which now showed a talking mop, jogging around someone's kitchen floor, each step leaving a dazzling sparkle.

She felt embarrassed whenever Mom appeared in a commercial as a sexy lady. Holly would much rather see her playing second fiddle to the talking mop, looking like a *normal* mother in ordinary clothes, and appearing in *their* kitchen instead of on television.

The front door, which Holly forgot to lock after all the times she'd promised her dad she'd keep it locked, burst open. Beth's frizzed-out blonde head appeared. "Hol-lee! The pasta is positively *petrified!*"

Holly bounced to her feet, not wanting to be asked why she was gagging to death on the living room floor.

Accustomed to Beth's exaggerations, she calmly gathered the sauce and a notebook, bit into the last carrot stick, clicked off the television, then followed her friend out the door.

Petrified, she assumed, was Beth's description of dried-out pasta noodles.

2

Holly followed Beth as she hopped off the side of the front porch into a pile of mushy snow, high-jumped over a low fence, then leapt onto the Tiptons' front porch.

It was a path they'd created to avoid having to run down sixteen steep steps from Holly's house, then up another sixteen steps to Beth's. There wasn't much flat land in all the city of Ketchikan, so many of the homes were built against the sloping hills.

Beth's older brother, Brian, greeted them at the front door. "What's going on in the kitchen? It smells like a forest fire on Mount McKinley."

"The rolls!" Beth shrieked, ducking under Brian's arm and dashing toward the kitchen. "Why didn't you take them out of the oven?"

Brian smirked at Holly in answer.

"Who's letting all that cold air into the house?" hollered Mrs. Tipton from upstairs, making Brian drop his arm and step back so Holly could pass.

"It's only Cheechako!" Brian yelled up the stairs. He thwacked Holly on the shoulder with a rubber band.

She ignored him, glad for the padded shoulders on her jacket. She rather liked the Alaskan Indian name Brian had given her. It was the natives' name for someone new to the state.

"Hi, Mrs. T!" Holly called. Beth's mom wrote novels in her second-floor office, and seemed to descend to ground level only when the manuscripts were ready to mail to the publisher.

Holly would have forgotten what Mrs. Tipton looked like if it weren't for the fact the entire family shared Beth's frizzy blonde hair, blue eyes, and stocky frame.

Beth called her into the kitchen. She was scooping almost-burnt rolls into a warmer. Her younger brother, Gary, was doing his homework at the table. "Gary pulled the rolls from the oven just in time."

Gary raised his head at the mention of his name. "What a stupendous guy."

Beth shoved a pan at her. "Start heating the sauce while I get the salmon ready."

Holly poured sauce into the pan and smiled at Gary, who was waiting for her reaction to his comment. He was ten months younger, a shorter, slighter version of Brian on the outside, but completely different from his brother on the inside.

Gary saved the rolls. Brian would have let them burn.

Although every girl at Ketchikan School seemed to be in love with Brian, the eighth-grade amateur actor who landed all the leading roles in school plays, Gary was the one Holly liked.

If anyone found out, she would absolutely die. Not even Beth could know. Nobody falls for a *younger* guy — especially a measly fifth-grader. The whole idea was ridiculous, which is why Holly kept it a secret.

"Can you girls destroy the kitchen quietly? I have to write a report on nocturnal animals." Gary grinned at them over a stack of books.

Great, Holly thought. Now Gary's using weird words like his sister.

"We're trying a new recipe we invented," Beth explained, "and we need the table so we can work on our Social Studies project. Can you study in your room?"

Holly wished Beth hadn't asked Gary to leave.

He let his science book fall shut. "What's on tonight's menu?"

"Salmon spaghetti," they both answered.

Gary moved to the stove and peeked under the lid. "You're going to ruin Holly's great Italian spaghetti sauce by putting fish into it?"

Beth nodded, and Holly absorbed the compliment.

8

"Why?"

"Because it hasn't been done before," Beth answered as if it were the stupidest question she'd ever heard.

"Why'd you make so much?"

"Half of it's for Holly's dad."

Gary put the lid back. "Sure hope you're using Italian fish," he said as he gathered his books and left.

Beth dumped the non-Italian salmon chunks into the sauce, then sat at the table, opening her notebook. "What are your ideas for our project?" she asked, reaching for a bowl of cookies.

Holly joined her at the table. "It seems obvious. What we do best is cook, right?" She waved away Beth's offer of cookies. Holly avoided junk food as vigorously as her friend consumed it. "So, we should turn our hobby into a business and open a restaurant."

"I agree, but it's got to be something different. Look at the restaurants around here. There are places for burgers, fried chicken, Mexican food, hot dogs, and Chinese food."

As she counted off each type of restaurant on her fingers, Holly joined in, "Cafeteria food, Thai, Japanese, and Mongolian food. Baked potatoes only, salads only, desserts only."

The more they listed, the less unique of an idea it seemed.

"You're right," Holly agreed. "We've got to

come up with a new twist, or we won't be able to stand the competition."

Beth strained to reach cookie number four. Holly slapped her hand away. "You won't eat the good meal we're preparing if you fill yourself up with junk food."

"Look, if I wanted a mother, I'd go upstairs." Beth gazed lovingly at the bowl, then carried it to a cupboard, shoving it out of sight. "Why can't good food taste as delicious as junk food?"

She licked stray crumbs off her fingers. "Why can't I get all the vitamins I need with no fat or cholesterol from a dinner of sugar cookies, butter brickle ice cream, and peppermint candy, with a slice of chocolate pudding cake on the side? Then, if anyone offered me vegetables for dessert, I could honestly say, 'No, *thank you*, *I* never *eat dessert!*' "

Holly laughed, recalling the time she'd caught her own dad stashing away store-bought cookies because she never baked desserts for him.

Suddenly she stopped laughing and jumped to her feet. "That's it! That's our twist, our something different!"

Beth returned to the table, hiding something under her sweater. "What is?"

"What type of junk food do you love the most?"

Beth sheepishly pulled a cookie from under her sweater and held it in front of her face.

"And what healthy food do you absolutely hate?"

She wrinkled her nose and shuddered. "Liver."

"So." Holly paced, cementing the plan in her head. "We take food that everyone knows is good for them, but they hate — like liver. Then we combine it with a junk food they love — like cookies."

She stopped and faced Beth. "We'll be creating food that not only *tastes* good, but is good *for* you."

Beth looked skeptical. "Like what?"

Holly grabbed the half-eaten cookie from Beth's hand, holding it up like a trophy. "Like Liver cookies!"

"Liver cookies?" Beth stared at her. "You're insane, Hol. That's so disgusting. No one will ever — "

"We'll make them tasty. I promise. We'll practice the recipe until we get it right." Holly dangled the half-cookie in front of Beth's face as bait. "Are you willing to try?"

Beth shrugged, snatching the cookie and swallowing it. "I've got one question."

"What?"

"After we *make* these cookies with liver" — she wrapped her arms around her stomach, pretending to be sick — "who's going to *eat* them?"

3

"**W**hen *you* want to be serious and mysterious," Holly recited along with her mother as she watched the commercial the next day after school. She'd taped it on her dad's VCR so she could watch it whenever she wanted. At least she could say she *saw* her mom every day.

There was no stigma to divorced parents, but hers weren't divorced.

They were separated.

Dad assured her he still loved Mom, but Mom hadn't said anything about still loving Dad. The thought gnawed at Holly's heart.

She watched the commercial a few more times, then clicked off the TV and went into the kitchen to heat leftover salmon spaghetti for dinner.

Holly wondered if Mom were dating. Mom never admitted to it, but she *had* told Holly to check out a certain guy in her new commercial, scheduled to air in a few days.

She seemed excited about working with this

guy, and called him *super jazzy*. She never used to talk like that in the old days. A little bit of Hollywood glitter must have rubbed off on her mother.

Holly knew Dad wasn't dating, but he did have a lady friend, as he called her. Parents were so corny sometimes, but Holly guessed it would be silly to call some thirty-year-old lady a *girl*friend.

They hadn't actually gone out on a date, as far as Holly knew, but Dad had spent hours sprawled across the hallway floor, talking to his friend on the telephone. It made Holly feel as if she were living with an overgrown teenager.

Adjusting the heat under the sauce, Holly prepared the pasta. While it was boiling, she took a broom from the closet to sweep stray noodles off the floor.

She danced around the kitchen, pretending the broom was the talkative jogging mop. "Makes my floor sparkle like a jewel!" she exclaimed, leaning over to catch her reflection in the not-very-sparkly floor.

"Holly Marie, you don't have to sweep the floor."

Holly jumped. She hadn't heard her dad come in. Quickly she shoved the broom back into the closet, and returned to the stove.

She hated Dad catching her doing something little girl-ish like this. Especially since he'd been so strict lately.

He crossed the kitchen in two steps and gave her a bear hug. Then he swung her around in a circle, her feet off the floor. His coat was wet from the rain, and the damp wool smell mingled with his woodsy after-shave. "Mrs. Kanaga comes in every week to clean. I'd rather you spent your time on homework."

Dad aimed a contented sniff in the direction of the stove. "I'm so glad one of us likes to cook, or we'd be in serious trouble."

He grinned, kissing her on the forehead, then stepped back to remove his overcoat and loosen his tie. "What are you doing Friday night?" He double-winked his eyes at her. It was a game they used to play when she was a little girl and could only wink one eye.

"Are you asking me on a date?" Holly teased. She hoped he wanted to take her to the Latitude 56 Restaurant for fresh seafood. Her favorite was lobster.

Her father's grin faded. "Um, no. I was hoping you'd make your famous Shipwreck casserole. I invited a friend to dinner."

Holly erased the thought of fresh lobster from her mind. "Okay, I guess." She tried not to sound disappointed. "Who's coming?"

Her dad began to pace the kitchen floor, which told Holly right away she was in for something unpleasant.

Hadn't he paced before he told her that her kitten had died?

Hadn't he paced when he announced they were moving to Alaska?

And, worst of all, hadn't he paced when he told her Mom wasn't moving with them?

Holly braced herself. What now? Were they moving to another *planet*?

Finally, Dad stopped and leaned against the refrigerator. "Um, I've invited a lady friend to dinner."

Holly let out the breath she'd been holding. She'd expected that for a long time. "It's okay," she said, trying to act as though it really were.

"Well, there's more." He began to pace again, running a hand through his short-cropped hair.

More? Holly held a pan suspended in midair. He invited his lady friend to dinner *and* they were moving to another planet?

"You know her."

"I do?" she asked in a weak voice. Holly prayed silently for it to be her mother.

He stopped pacing. "Yes. It's Marilyn, I mean, Ms. Frank."

"Ms. Frank?" Holly's throat tightened so much she could hardly get the words out. "You mean *my* Ms. Frank? My music teacher at school?"

Her dad nodded.

Holly felt sick. How could her own dad be

15

friends behind her back with her music teacher, of all people?

Methodically carrying dinner to the table, Holly hoped if she acted normal, maybe her father would laugh and say he was only joking.

He didn't.

He sat at the table and dished up his plate, so Holly did the same, studying her food as if she'd never seen salmon spaghetti leftovers before. Of course she hadn't, but that was beside the point.

She thought over Dad's announcement. It wasn't that she disliked her music teacher. Holly *did* like her. Ms. Frank was from Germany, and had taught her students German phrases and songs.

But Ms. Frank and her mother were hundreds of miles apart — literally as well as otherwise.

Ms. Frank was pumpkin pie, but Mom was the whipped cream on top. Ms. Frank was vanilla ice cream, while Mom was raspberry twirl. Ms. Frank was decaffeinated coffee. Mom was mocha mint.

"Holly Marie, are you all right?" Her dad's voice dissolved her daydream.

"Sure." Holly realized she'd been going through the motions of eating dinner, yet hadn't tasted anything.

Dad leaned toward her. His eyebrows wrinkled. "Is it school?"

"School's fine."

"Is it Beth?"

"Beth's fine."

"Are you upset with me for inviting your teacher to dinner?"

"No," she lied. "It's okay."

"Then is it . . . ?"

Oh, jeez. Holly groaned to herself. She could tell by the look on Dad's face what was coming. For the past few months, he'd been trying to play the role of *Mother* so he could prepare her for getting her first period. Unfortunately, it had come long before his attempts to prepare her.

"Have you . . . ?"

"Yes, Dad." She'd been too embarrassed to tell him before, but maybe if she told him now, he'd quit bringing it up.

"You have?" His voice was full of surprise. "When?"

"Last January, right after we moved here."

A melancholy look clouded his face, as if she'd told him she was twenty-five years old, married with two kids, and he hadn't even noticed time had passed. "Are you having any problems?"

"No, Dad."

"Well, Holly, sometimes you may feel, um, depressed or upset, or — "

"I know."

"You know already?"

"Yes, Dad. Mrs. Kanaga told me."

With that he came around to her side of the

table and knelt by the chair. He pulled Holly to him and hugged her so tightly she had to hold her breath. "You know you can talk to me about things like this."

Holly rubbed her cheek up and down against his ear in a nod, unsure of her own voice.

"My little girl is growing up." His words were muffled in her hair.

"Da-ad," Holly mumbled, wishing he'd stop with the little girl stuff.

A shudder went through her at the remembrance of how angry she'd been at her mom for not being here the first time her period had come, and how miserable she'd felt going to Mrs. Kanaga with her questions.

Holly meant to push her dad away, but instead hugged him back. Burying her head in his strong shoulder, she began to cry.

4

"I can't believe I'm spending my allowance on liver," Beth grumbled as the two girls hurried toward the meat department at the grocery store.

Holly stopped to study the long freezer of packaged meats and wondered where the liver might be.

Beth bumped into her. "Do you think the meat's lined up alphabetically?" she asked. "Like, albacore, then bologna, chicken, duck, eel — ?"

"This isn't the library. We can't go to the card file and look under L for liver," Holly glanced at her friend. "Did you say *eel*?"

Beth ran her hand along the edge of the freezer. "I couldn't think of a meat that started with E. Do people eat eel?"

"I don't know. Maybe we can try it in a recipe. How about eel enchiladas?"

"Ugh." Beth made a face. "Come on. I think I see the liver."

They stopped under a sign that said THE MEAT-

19

ING PLACE, and leaned over the freezer. "Gross," they chimed in unison at the packages of brown slime before them.

"Why are there three sizes?" Beth whispered, shooting a guilty glance around the meat department as if the butcher might send them to the principal's office for looking at liver.

Holly leaned further to read the packages. "The big one is a cow's liver. The medium one is a pig's, and the little ones are chicken livers."

"Let's get the little ones."

"Why?"

"If I have to touch the yucky things, I'd rather they were tiny."

They picked out the cheapest package and carried it to the express lane.

"Find everything all right?" the lady checker asked, acting as if hundreds of sixth-graders had gone through her line tonight, buying packages of chicken livers.

Returning to Beth's house, Holly jotted ingredients for a basic cookie recipe in her notebook, while Beth pulled supplies from the cupboard, setting bags of white flour, sugar, and salt in a neat row on the counter.

"Hold it," Holly said. "We're not going to use that kind of stuff in our cookies."

Beth raised an eyebrow. "What do you mean, *that kind of stuff*? This is what cookies are made of."

"We have to use *healthy* ingredients, like wheat flour, honey, oat bran, and salt substitute."

"We don't have any of those things." Beth stretched to her toes, checking a higher cupboard. "These are all the staples we have."

Holly dropped her pencil onto the table in exasperation. "We're not going to use *staples* in our cookies. What do you think that gives you? Extra iron?"

She felt warm, waiting for Beth to stop laughing.

"Staples are things like flour, salt, and sugar." Beth flopped onto a chair. "Wait till I tell Brian what you said. He'll love it."

Holly hoped Beth would forget about it before her brother got home. He loved shooting them down. Why give him more ammunition?

Wildly scratching out the recipe, she started over. "Doesn't your mother cook with healthy ingredients?"

"My mother comes downstairs on holidays, or to go to the post office. My dad comes home on weekends because of his sales job. Haven't you figured it out yet? The only reason I *like* to cook is because I *have* to cook. My brothers and I would never eat if I didn't."

Holly felt a twinge of envy. Her mother didn't cook for her either, but at least Beth's mom was a staircase away, not hundreds of miles away. "Sorry," she said.

"It's okay. I've got another idea. Let's make the cookies with a mix this time so we can experiment with the liver. It'll work for a trial run." Beth pulled a box off the shelf. "Can we use chocolate?"

"Why?"

"It's brown. The liver won't show."

Gingerly, Beth unwrapped the package of meat. "Do we cook it first or throw it in raw?"

"I don't know." Holly had wondered the same thing. "Let's divide the batter and try both ways." She threw a few pieces of meat into a pan to cook. The rest she chopped into teeny tiny bits as Beth peered over her shoulder. Chopping limp liver was difficult — especially with an audience.

Holly slid the cookies into the oven, then quickly washed her hands. This whole thing *had* been her idea, and she wanted to maintain her enthusiasm in front of Beth. But still, it was eerie to know liver lurked inside the cookie batter, like a crafty enemy lying in wait to attack one's taste buds on the very first bite.

"Okay," Holly said, drying her hands. "Let's get started on the outline for our new business."

Beth leaned against the counter. "We need a location."

"How about Front Street where the cruise ships dock? There are always a lot of people there."

Beth nodded. "Next, the menu."

"Look how long it's taking us to come up with our first recipe." Holly motioned toward the oven where the cookies rose like hatching baby monsters in a horror movie. "It'll take forever to develop recipes for breakfast, lunch, and dinner."

Beth ripped open a bag of Oreos. "Why can't we serve *normal* food?"

"Because we have to have a hook — something that's never been done before. We have to build a better mousetrap."

"Why?"

"So the world will beat a pathway to our door."

Beth twisted an Oreo apart. "How'd you learn all this?"

The image of her mother spraying perfume toward the television camera flashed through Holly's mind. "I watch a lot of commercials."

"But, Hol, what about Famous Amos? He sells only — "

"That's it!"

The oven timer buzzed.

"Beth, you're a genius." Holly removed the cookies with pot-holdered hands. "Famous Amos is successful because he sells *only* cookies."

"That's what I started to say. Then there's Mrs. Fields cookies, and — "

"Taco Bell serves Mexican food. Kentucky Fried serves chicken. Wendy's specializes in . . . mmmmmf."

Beth had shoved a warm Liver cookie into Holly's mouth. Holly started to bite it in two, then had second thoughts. She yanked the cookie from her mouth, giving her friend a sheepish smile.

"Hol, are you suggesting we serve *only* Liver cookies? We'll go broke. People might spend money on chocolate chips — but not on liver chunks."

"No. We'll serve *snacks*. Healthy junk snacks.

"Healthy junk snacks?" Beth repeated. "Wait till Brian hears — "

"We'll give our customers a variety. All of it will *look* like junk food, but will be much healthier — like the Liver cookies."

"And what else?" Beth sounded unsure.

Holly swung open the refrigerator door. She dropped to her knees and inventoried the bottom shelf, then rose, a bag of fresh broccoli in one hand and a can of diet cola in the other. "How about Broccoli cola?"

Beth laughed. "You can't be serious." She scooped the two kinds of Liver cookies into separate bowls.

Holly washed the broccoli and dumped it into Mrs. Tipton's food chopper. Above the whirring sound she hollered, "This cola has no caffeine, no sugar, no salt, and now, thanks to us, it has vitamins and fiber."

Holly felt pleased with her newest invention as she spooned the smushed broccoli into a tall glass, pouring cola over it.

"Ta-da!" She held her hand on top of the glass and gave it a vigorous shake. Sipping it, she licked her lips, then cocked her head toward Beth, pretending she was starring in a commercial. "Broccoli cola. It's the right thing to drink."

Beth grabbed Holly's arm to steady it, then chanced a sip. "Wow, you can barely tell there's broccoli in here, thanks to the food chopper."

Holly plunked the glass onto the table and arranged the two bowls of cookies in an inviting fashion on a place mat. "Well, if you think Broccoli cola is a success, then all we need now is an unsuspecting victim — "

She slapped one hand over her mouth, catching her mistake. "I mean, an unsuspecting *customer*, to test-taste our Liver cookies."

"I'm home, Mom!" came Gary's voice from the living room as the front door slammed behind him.

5

"Hello, Elizabeth," Gary said, tugging at Beth's hair as he stepped into the kitchen. He nodded at Holly, dumped his schoolbooks onto the table, picked up a raw Liver cookie, and stuffed it into his mouth before either girl could say a word.

"Who made these?" he asked in a muffled voice, grabbing a cooked Liver cookie and wolfing it down as fast as the first one.

The girls stared, then pointed at each other to answer his question.

Holly was hypnotized, watching Gary eat the Liver cookies, one after the other. She expected him to grab his stomach, rush to the bathroom — or die. She didn't expect him simply to stand there and keep eating them.

Holly moved closer. "Well?"

"Well, what?"

"Which taste better? The cookies from bowl

number one?" she asked, pointing. "Or the cookies from bowl number two?"

Gary smoothed his unsmoothable hair, pivoting in the middle of the kitchen. "Okay, where's the hidden camera? Am I on television?"

Stopping mid-turn, he pointed toward bowl number two — the cooked Liver cookies. "These do have a strange aftertaste, now that you've asked. What kind of cookies are they?"

Holly and Beth exchanged looks. Who was going to tell him? Beth took a deep breath and patted Holly on the shoulder, as if to say it would be better for a blood relative to relay the gross news to Gary.

"They're Liver cookies."

"They're what?"

Holly wondered if Gary would be mad at her. She watched as Beth sat him down at the table, a bit motherly. "Holly will explain it to you," she said.

Thanks, friend. I want your brother to like me, not think I'm trying to poison him.

Clearing her throat, Holly told Gary about their Social Studies project.

Much to her surprise, he studied his last bite of cookie like a scientist would study an alien life-form. Sniffing at it, he popped it into his mouth. Then he made a face the same scientist might make as he realizes the alien life-form is planning to swallow him whole.

"Give me something to wash this down."

Holly grabbed the Broccoli cola and handed it to him. He chugged half of it, choked, then peered suspiciously into the glass. "Why are there tiny green things floating in my drink?"

She took a deep breath, sure she'd made him mad now. "It's Broccoli cola."

Gary collapsed onto the table. "I've just eaten liver and broccoli for my after-school snack. Mother will be so pleased."

He moaned. "Stand back, I'm about to die."

"You're not about to die," Holly said. "Healthy junk snacks are good for you."

Gary lifted his head. "Is that what you call them? Healthy junk snacks?"

Holly nodded. *Here it comes*, she thought.

But instead of getting angry, Gary grinned. "This is great," he said, holding the glass up to study it. "Can I help?"

Beth and Holly exchanged looks again.

"Sure," Beth answered. "You can be our new official taste-tester."

"What happened to your *old* official taste-tester?"

"He died of unknown causes." Beth sang the theme from *The Twilight Zone*, "Do do do do. Do do do — "

"Stop it," Holly scolded.

"What if eating your recipes makes hair grow all over my body?"

Holly grinned at him. "Then you'll be the warmest person in Alaska."

Gary's laugh warmed her as much as the hot oven warmed the kitchen.

"Let's get down to business," he said, taking over Holly's notebook. "Have you made up a slogan?"

Beth shook her head. "We haven't gotten that far."

He thought for a moment. "How about, *Liver Cookies — when you care enough to eat the very best.*"

Beth sprinkled cookie crumbs onto her tongue. "I don't think that will work. I don't think calling our snack stand *Liver Cookies, Incorporated*, will work, either. That will turn kids off."

"I've got it!" Gary exclaimed. "*McLiver!*"

Beth pretended to choke on the crumbs.

"Let's think of something light and kicky," Holly began, borrowing words from her mother's commercial. "How about *HJ's*? Everyone will think it's short for someone's name, but the three of us will know it means Healthy Junk Snacks."

"I like it," Gary said, and Beth agreed.

Holly mixed Broccoli colas for everyone, then passed around the Liver cookies. The three new partners sang *The Twilight Zone* theme in unison as they lifted their glasses to toast the birth of HJ's.

6

Holly tiptoed to a folding chair in the back of the KKAL television studio. The camera blocked her view of the anchor team presenting the five o'clock news, so she scooted the chair to one side. It scraped against the floor, making the camera technician whip around and shush her. Then the tech pointed toward the ON THE AIR sign above the door.

It was fun to watch the news live and the TV monitor at the same time. When a commercial appeared on the screen for the home audience, the news team relaxed and joked around. When the commercial was over, the camera tech counted backward, signaling the team to get serious again and pose for the camera.

Holly thought her father was better-looking than the man giving the weather report, but Dad stayed behind the scenes since he was producer of the news.

She wondered if he ever regretted the day back

home when his old station needed a *new face* to tape commercials for KLTV. Dad had volunteered Mom, who, at first, was reluctant and scared.

The talent agency coordinating the commercial worked on Mom for an entire morning. They styled her hair, dressed her in glamorous clothes, gave her quick acting lessons, then placed her in front of the camera.

What happened then was magic. The instant the cameras rolled, Mom lost all her fear. She blossomed right there in the studio, turning the memorized lines of the commercial into a performance worthy of an award.

One of the talent coordinators told Holly that her mom's talent had been simmering under the surface "like a genie bottled up for five hundred years."

Mom was never quite the same after that. No longer was she Jackie. Now she was Jacqueline. The agency offered a contract, then signed her with the Screen Actors Guild. A photographer followed her around for three days, snapping pictures for a portfolio.

Over the next few weeks Holly's sweats-and-blue jeans mom was transformed into a high-fashion model and actress.

Holly came out of her daydream to wave at Dad as he crossed the studio to speak with the camera tech.

Dad tapped his watch, then held up ten fingers,

meaning the news would be over in ten minutes and they could leave. Tonight was his turn to cook, so he'd offered her an Eskimo burger on the way home.

Holly fell back into the daydream about her mother as the sports announcer predicted scores for the upcoming weekend. Mom's transition had frightened her. Holly was only nine at the time, and up until then, she always had her mother's undivided attention.

As Mom became busy with bookings and auditions, Holly got lost in the shuffle. Her mom kept saying, "Isn't this great? Isn't this marvelous?" She even teased about changing Holly's middle name to Wood, so she'd be Holly Wood, instead of Holly Marie.

Holly was glad it was only a joke. Her mom had become so unpredictable, she might actually have done it.

When it all first began, Holly was proud of Mom, but she sensed that something was bound to go wrong. It felt as if the earth were shifting, the way it does in L.A. during their frequent tremors.

Mom didn't look, walk, or talk like herself anymore. Working for the agency had changed her, as if by a fairy godmother's magic wand. Only this time, Cinderella never came home from the ball.

Dad changed, too. He became much quieter. He was the one who'd introduced Mom to her new life, but still, Holly believed he missed Mom the way she used to be, just as Holly did.

"Ready?" came Dad's voice from behind.

Holly pulled on her coat and followed him across the studio as everyone waved good-bye. The camera tech who'd shushed her earlier opened the door. "Pretty daughter you've got there, Mr. Mann," the tech said. "She should be on the other side of the camera."

Her dad gave an unconvincing chuckle as they stepped through the door. He shot Holly a look as if to warn, *"Don't you dare even consider it."*

A hint of sadness flickered in his eyes as he nudged her on the cheek with his fist and said, "One Mann in front of the camera is enough. I couldn't take it if both my girls turned into Hollywood stars."

As much as she envied her mom's glamorous life, being a star was the last thing on Holly's mind. She'd rather be the manager of HJ's. She'd rather be an entrepreneur.

"I told Brian about HJ's last night," Beth informed Holly the next morning as they waited to enter the school building. "He says it's impossible for two girls to start their own business."

"I would expect Brian to say something like that."

"He says we're going to fail and lose a lot of money."

"We're *not* going to fail." Holly wasn't sure of

33

her words, but she vowed to give it her best shot, just to prove Brian wrong.

"I think he's right." Beth pulled a piece of paper from her pocket. "Here are the questions I asked the mayor's secretary about opening HJ's on Front Street."

Beth handed the paper to her. "And here are the answers." She pointed to the list of *NOs* down the right margin.

Holly leaned against the brick wall of the school to study the paper. It was all there in black and white.

They were too young to get a sales license or permission from the board of health to open a snack stand. And, rent on Front Street was outrageous, according to Beth's figures. They'd never be able to afford anything, including a miniature lemonade stand.

Holly could feel Beth's eyes on her as she read. "So?" she asked.

"What do you mean, *so*?" Beth stepped from the path of a vigorous game of keep away. "That's it. We can't do it. It's a stalemate."

"A what?" Holly's head ached every time she had to ask Beth for a translation.

"A dead end. We're going to get an F. We — "

"Okay, okay. I get the point." Holly crumpled the piece of paper. "So, we simply go on to plan B."

"I didn't know we *had* a plan B."

The first bell rang.

"Sure we do."

"Well, what is it?"

Holly nudged Beth toward the sixth-grade line.

"I'll let you know as soon as I think one up."

7

That night, Holly hurried through the dishes, eager to get to Beth's so they could work out the final recipe for Liver cookies. She dialed the Tipton's number with one hand, while hanging up a dish towel with the other. "Hi, are you ready to — ?"

"Hello, this is Eliza," came Beth's voice.

Holly was confused for a moment, then remembered her friend's hobby of changing the form of her name whenever the mood struck. She'd been *Beth* when they met, so that's what Holly continued to call her.

At the time, Beth had been reading *Little Women*, and became convinced she was dying from the same ailment plaguing the girl in the book.

Shortly after that, their Social Studies class read a story about Betsy Ross, so Beth decided she wasn't dying anymore, became *Betsy*, and wore red, white, and blue to school every day.

Then, an actress named Elizabeth gained stardom, so Beth became *Elizabeth*, and started acting like a movie star.

"So, why Eliza?"

"Oh, Holly, we went to see Brian's play last night at school. It's *Pygmalion*, and it's about Doctor Doolittle, and — "

"And there's a character in the play named Eliza," Holly finished for her, glad Beth hadn't changed her name to Doolittle.

"How'd you guess?"

Holly laughed in answer. "I'll be right over." She hung up the phone and grabbed her notes with scribbled bits of recipes. Slinging a rain parka over her shoulders, she took the shortcut to Beth's porch, dashing through the rain.

Holly wished her own name were a fancy one she could shorten or lengthen at will. She was just plain Holly, born on Christmas Eve. She wondered how many other Hollys in the world were named after the same season.

Beth met her at the door. "I've got all the healthy ingredients we were missing last time we made the cookies."

"Great," Holly answered, following Beth to the kitchen. "I worked out the recipe for Broccoli cola. Two recipes down, how many more to go?"

"Good question. Maybe five or six would be about right for HJ's."

The door slammed, announcing Gary's late arrival. He rushed into the kitchen, face flushed from the freezing drizzle. "Have you mixed the cookies yet, Beth?"

"It's Eliza," she answered.

Gary rolled his eyes and played along. "Have you mixed the cookies yet, *Eliza*?"

"No. I'm not in any hurry to get my hands into the squishy liver again."

"I've got something better."

"There are a *lot* of things better than liver, little brother."

Gary wiggled out of his jacket, pulling a brown bag from the pocket. "After school, I stopped at the Bayside Deli for a snack. A lady was handing out sample hors d'oeuvres."

"Or what?"

Holly snickered. *At last! A word not even Beth knows.*

"Hors d'oeuvres," Gary repeated. "Appetizers. This brown gunk called *pâté* was smeared onto crackers. It smelled real familiar, so I asked the lady what it was, and she said pâté was smushed-up liver.

"So, stupendous guy that I am, I bought some so you don't have to chop liver anymore."

Gary set the pâté on the counter. "I can't believe I spent my allowance on liver."

The girls laughed at his familiar words.

Brian wandered into the kitchen. "What are you

little children up to this afternoon?"

No one offered an explanation.

He investigated on his own, peeling off the lid on the pâté, then covering his nose. "*What* are you doing?"

"We're cooking," Gary explained.

Brian grabbed Gary from behind and wrestled with him. "*Girls* cook," he hollered. "Guys don't."

Holly bit her lip to keep from commenting.

Gary wriggled away. "Come on, Bri."

Brian ruffled Gary's hair. "I won't let any brother of mine grow up to be a geek."

"He's not a geek." Beth spun her big brother toward the doorway, then gave him a light shove.

"I'll defend myself, Eliza, thank you very much." Gary gave Brian a shove of his own. "I'm *not* a geek."

"Who's Eliza?" Brian looked confused.

The others laughed, then began to mix the Liver cookies with pâté.

Ignored, Brian gave up. "I'm going out. Can I get anything at the store for you, little sister?"

"No." Beth smiled at him. "But thanks for asking."

Holly watched as Brian affectionately squeezed his sister's shoulders. The sight tweaked a little place in Holly's heart left empty by the absence of her mom.

Her parents had been talking about having a

baby right up until the time they separated. She wondered what it would be like to have two brothers like Gary and Brian.

Holly jumped as Brian unexpectedly squeezed her shoulders, too.

"Hey, little Cheechako, you're here so much, you're like one of the family."

He gave her a gorgeous smile. "But you'll have to dye your hair blonde and get it frizzed if you want to fit into the Tipton family."

Charmer, Holly thought, as Beth and Gary chuckled.

Brian pointed a finger at her. "You call me, now, if my brother starts acting like a geek, okay? And I'll come home and straighten him out."

"Good-bye, Brian," Holly waved a cookbook at him.

Gary lifted the spoon from the mixing bowl. Gooey clumps of batter dripped onto the counter.

He held it out to his brother. "Want to lick the spoon?"

"Hey, thanks." Brian's eyes lit up at Gary's generosity. He took the spoon and left, noisily lapping up liver batter.

8

Holly pulled the umbrella low until it rested on top of her head. She leapt from the school bus and dashed down the street, keeping her eyes on the rain-soaked sidewalk. Her saturated tennis shoes squished with each footfall.

After dashing up the cement steps, she hopped on one foot, then the other, pulling off her soggy shoes so she wouldn't track mud inside.

It was hard getting used to the monotonous Alaskan rain. California offered a lot more sunshine. Alaskans sometimes called their daily precipitation *liquid* sunshine.

"See you tomorrow!" Holly yelled at Beth, who was dashing up the steps to her own house.

Beth hollered something in answer, but Holly couldn't hear it. Wind gusted the rain sideways in waves, almost as if someone were standing offstage throwing buckets of water at her.

Holly collapsed the umbrella and stepped inside. She wasn't superstitious about open um-

41

brellas, but Mrs. Kanaga was, and it was her day to clean house for the Manns.

Taking off her raincoat and hat, Holly left them in the entryway. The smell of brownies led her to the kitchen.

Mrs. Kanaga was pulling a pan from the oven. She smiled at Holly. "I thought I'd help out with the special dinner you're making tonight." Setting the hot pan on top of the stove, she cut the brownies into bars, then scooped them onto a plate to cool.

Holly hated to be reminded that it was Friday night — the night Ms. Frank was coming to dinner. But it was typical of Mrs. Kanaga to help.

"Thanks." Holly snitched a warm brownie, then hugged the grandmotherly Mrs. Kanaga. Her own grandmothers died long ago, and she didn't remember either one of them. But Holly imagined they'd have been just like Mrs. Kanaga.

Except for their hair.

No one had hair like the housekeeper's. It was the color of ashes — black, tinged with gray — and hung well past her knees. She tied it at the nape of her neck, letting it fall straight as rain down her back.

Mrs. Kanaga winked at her. "If you steal a dessert before dinner, you'll have bad luck before the day is over."

Holly figured her luck couldn't get much worse than having to cook dinner for her music teacher.

"Would you like me to stay and help with the rest of the meal?" Mrs. Kanaga asked.

"No." Holly licked her fingers and reached for another brownie. Double bad luck. But sometimes junk food tasted pretty good, she decided, glad Beth wasn't here to see what she was eating.

She wondered what health food she could doctor this dessert with. Asparagus brownies? Brownie à la halibut? Brownies with tofu?

"No," she repeated, remembering Mrs. Kanaga's question. "Dad told Ms. Frank I was preparing dinner all by myself, so I can't disappoint him."

"Well, then, I'll be leaving. Two cooks in one kitchen means a baby will fall ill before dusk."

Holly hugged Mrs. Kanaga good-bye, wondering if the proverb worked when there were no babies around.

Hurrying upstairs, she dried her rain-wet hair, then put on the dress Dad had given her when school started. Holly liked it, even though she hadn't worn it yet. On a cold Ketchikan morning, it made more sense to reach for a pair of heavy corduroy pants, socks, and a sweater than panty hose and a flimsy dress.

She stood in front of the bedroom mirror and brushed her hair. It blended nicely with the cinnamon-colored dress, looking as though it were the same color.

"Goes with everything," Holly exclaimed, wide-

43

eyed, pretending she was modeling the dress for a commercial. She twirled in front of the mirror, making the calf-length skirt fan out.

"You can wear it to school, to the fish hatcheries, or to the docks. It's completely water-repellent; you needn't carry an umbrella on rainy days." She cocked her head the way her mother did on television. "Brought to you by the makers of — *Rain Dresses.*"

Holly stuck her tongue out at her reflection in the mirror, then hurried downstairs to start dinner.

It was almost time for Mom's new commercial, so, as promised, Holly quickly prepared her dad's favorite — Shipwreck casserole — and slid it into the oven. She put a cube of butter into the microwave to soften for the rolls, then hurried to the living room and turned on the television. Watching commercials seemed to be her latest hobby.

Holly moved the wooden rocker in front of the TV so she wouldn't have to sit on the floor in her dress.

Today's commercial lineup started with a talking walrus selling sunglasses. Then, two pairs of long underwear danced in front of a fireplace at a ski lodge. Lastly, an animated slice of bread dared her to eat it.

Finally a human appeared. A handsome man, who looked a little bit like her dad, told her how soft and kissable her skin would be if she used super-fatted Chinchilla soap.

Chinchilla soap! This was it — Mom's newest commercial.

Holly sat spellbound. The handsome man opened the door to a steam-filled bathroom as he talked about the virtues of the soap.

The camera zoomed into the room. There, in the shower, was her mom, grasping what Holly assumed was the wonderful Chinchilla soap, and lathering it in tiny circles over her bare shoulder.

Mom laughed joyously at the camera, as if taking a shower were more fun than Disneyland.

"Mother!"

Holly stopped the rocker. "Mo-ther!"

What was her mom doing taking a shower on television? That was *much* worse than getting carried into the mist in the arms of a tuxedo-wearing stranger.

And who was this man standing there in the bathroom with her?

Was this Mr. Super Jazzy?

She clicked off the TV before the commercial ended, not wanting to see if the man demonstrated how soft and kissable her mother's skin was.

Holly began to pace — a lot like her dad paced. Only she kicked the rocker each time she passed it.

"Why can't you advertise kitchen cleanser? (Kick) Or breakfast cereal? (Kick) Or — or cat food? (Kick) At least you'd have to wear *clothes* in those commercials."

Suddenly Holly wanted to talk to her mother. It had been a long time since Mom had called because it was expensive.

But it didn't matter. Holly needed to hear her voice.

What if her mom liked the man in the soap commercial? She'd told Holly to check him out, hadn't she? What if she were dating him? The man looked just like Dad, *that's* why Mom liked him. Holly knew it.

She pulled Mom's phone number out of the secret compartment in her book bag where she kept it. What if Mom were out on a date with the soap man right now?

And Dad was having his first date with her music teacher tonight?

"This is *not* the way things are supposed to happen!" Holly yelled at the blank TV screen. She picked up the phone, punching the numbers with her knuckle as hard as she could.

The line crackled sympathetically in Holly's ear, as if it knew just how far Los Angeles was from Ketchikan.

"Hello?" said a voice, not really sounding all that far away.

"Mom?"

"Holly? Is this Holly?" Her mom's voice

sounded pleased, making Holly relax and sink into the nearest chair.

She'd half expected Mom's answering machine to click on and say, *"I'm not home right now. I'm out on a date with the super jazzy guy I film soap commercials with. If you want to date me, too, please leave your number after the tone."*

"Hello?" came her mother's voice again, sounding concerned.

"Hi, Mom."

Holly wished she'd thought about what she was going to say after she called. Hearing Mom say her name made her feel better.

"Honey, are you all right? Is anything wrong?"

Mom's worried questions secretly pleased her. *Let her worry. Let her catch the next plane to Alaska and fly up here to make darn sure her only child is all right.*

"Yes, I'm fine. How are you?"

It was an expensive call for small talk, Holly reminded herself. "I just saw your new commercial."

"You did? How'd you like it?"

"Wel-l-l-l." Should she be honest? "Mom, did you have to film a commercial in the shower?"

"It was a *soap* commercial. Where did you want me to be? At a rodeo?"

"No."

Her mom groaned. "I expected to have this conversation with your father, not with you." She shuffled the phone, and Holly knew she was pulling off an earring because that's how she started all her phone conversations these days — now that she wore earrings.

"Honey, what you see through the camera is an illusion. I was wearing a body suit the whole time. It wasn't any different from filming other commercials, except I had to stand in water all day with wet hair. My hands were as wrinkled as California raisins from lathering Chinchilla soap for eight hours, plus I caught a cold."

"What about the man?"

"What man?"

"The soap man."

"Oh, *that* man. Sam."

Holly didn't like the way she said his name. Why couldn't it be *Mr*. Sam?

"Is he . . . ? Are you . . . ?"

"What, Holly?"

"Are you dating him?"

Mom laughed. What kind of an answer was that?

"He's married."

Holly had never been happier to hear two words in her whole life.

"Holly Marie." Mom's voice softened. "I'm not dating anyone. Dating is the last thing on my mind. Besides, I'm not divorced. Your father and I are separated. And, Holly," she added in a quiet voice, "I still love him very much."

Holly had never been happier to hear those words, either, however many they were.

"Your father isn't dating anyone else," Mom said.

When Holly didn't answer right away, she added, "Is he?"

Holly detected a worried quiver in her voice. She glanced at the clock. Ms. Frank would be here in one hour. Until then, her dad hadn't actually dated anyone else.

"No," she answered truthfully.

"Well, see?" Her mom sounded relieved. "Maybe he still likes me a little bit, too."

"Oh, Mom, I know he does. He loves you and misses you, and" — suddenly she felt as if she were doing something behind her dad's back she shouldn't be doing — "and so do I," she finished.

"I love you, too, Holly Marie. And this call must be costing a fortune, so we'd better say good-bye. Take care, honey. I miss you."

"Bye, Mom."

Holly hung up the phone and curled into the chair. She knew Dad wanted Mom to come back. Now all she had to do was convince Mom of the same thing. But she couldn't do it over the phone. She needed to convince her in person.

Holly wondered how much a plane ticket to Los Angeles cost. When HJ's started making money, she would save her share and buy a plane ticket.

"Yes," Holly said out loud, liking the idea the more she thought about it. "I'll fly home for Christmas vacation and talk Mom into coming back to Alaska with me."

Holly closed her eyes, trying to imagine what it would be like to return to California. She'd almost forgotten how warm the afternoon sun felt on her face, how a palm tree rustled in the breeze, and how sweet her mom's yellow rose garden smelled.

Holly breathed in.

The air here didn't smell at all like yellow roses.

It smelled an awful lot like burning Shipwreck casserole.

9

Holly dashed into the kitchen and yanked open the oven door. The smoking cheese on top of her Shipwreck casserole was blackened instead of melted.

Grabbing two pot holders, she jerked the dish from the oven, knowing there was no need to rush. The damage was already done.

She slammed the gurgling dish onto the stove top, then hurled the pot holders across the room.

Ruined, she thought.

Shipwrecked.

Snatching up a spoon, she mushed the top of the casserole, trying to hide the black cheese and make the dish look more appetizing. The more she mushed, the worse it looked.

What should she do? She didn't have time to start over. Maybe she could melt more cheese. But when Holly opened the microwave, she found the forgotten cube of butter she'd intended to soften.

It had transformed into a greasy puddle, spreading out toward the open door. Now there wouldn't be any butter for the rolls, or time to melt cheese after cleaning the microwave.

She slumped into a chair at the kitchen table. Dad would be home any second, bringing her teacher, who'd smiled at her all during music class today.

Ms. Frank had said Dad raved about her cooking. *Eine gut Köchin*, she'd called Holly. *A good cook*.

Holly wondered how to say, *Ha, ha. The surprise is on you*, in German.

"At least Ms. Frank will never come back to dinner again," she said to herself. The thought made her bolt upright in her chair. "Never come back to dinner again! If I serve a horrible dinner, she'll never come back. Then I won't have to worry about her and Dad anymore."

It was a brilliant idea.

Holly put water on the stove to boil for tea. But instead of two tea bags, she slipped in six. Pausing, she threw in a seventh for good measure.

She tossed a salad, but *forgot* to put in lettuce — accidentally on purpose. Then she mixed oil and vinegar for dressing, and *forgot* to put in the oil.

Holly left lumps in the mashed potatoes, oversalted the gravy, and *forgot* to add yeast to the rolls. They looked like dead pancakes.

Ruining dinner was fun.

Holly imagined herself posing before a television camera on a drizzling Alaskan night, looking mysterious, wrapped in a raincoat.

Pulling her rain hat low, she peered into the camera. Then, in her spookiest voice, she uttered to the audience at home:

"It began as any ordinary Friday night dinner, but for one Marilyn Frank, it was a dinner she would never forget. For Marilyn Frank had unknowingly entered . . . The Twilight Zone. *Do do do do, do do do — "*

"Holly Marie?"

Holly whipped around, knocking over the now-empty saltshaker.

"Dad!" She felt her cheeks color.

Did Dad look a little embarrassed? Or was it her imagination? He probably wanted to say, "No, this isn't my daughter. I don't know who this weird girl is. *My* daughter must be upstairs."

Instead, he said, "Do you always sing while you're cooking?"

Ms. Frank came through the kitchen door behind him, smiling.

Holly prayed the teacher hadn't heard what she'd said. Suddenly feeling shy, she turned back to the stove, unsure of how to act.

It was strange seeing Dad and her teacher in the same room, knowing it wasn't because she'd gotten into trouble at school.

"Well, is this the way you greet your old dad?" he asked, holding out his arms.

Holly dropped a spoon and stepped across the room into his hug, hanging on as he swung her around in a circle. She felt relieved that she could act normal in front of their guest.

She also felt a little smug that her dad hadn't overlooked their daily hugging ritual just because his lady friend was here.

Holly kissed his cheek. He seemed to be wearing more after-shave than usual. She didn't approve.

While she was hugging him, she glanced at Ms. Frank, who looked like herself, only better. Her hair was loose, instead of tied back like she wore it at school, and she was wearing jeans and a sweatshirt that said HUG A TEACHER.

Holly wondered if she was supposed to hug Ms. Frank, too, or if the message was there for her dad's benefit. She didn't approve.

"What's that terrible smell?" Dad asked, pulling away.

"Dinner."

He paused a beat, giving her a worried glance. "Well, if you ladies will excuse me, I'll get rid of this tie and jacket."

Holly watched him leave, wondering why she'd bothered to put on a dress.

"Is there anything I can do to help?" Ms. Frank asked.

Yes, go home.

"No," Holly answered, wanting her teacher to see how well she could handle everything herself.

She flew around the kitchen, setting the table, lighting two candles, and even remembering the fancy napkins with the little ducks on them.

Feeling good all of a sudden, she decided to impress Ms. Frank with a bit of German she remembered from class by offering her a chair.

"Mochten Sie einen Hund?" she asked politely, scooting a chair from the table.

Ms. Frank gave her an odd look and continued to stand. "No, thank you," she answered. "I already have a dog."

"Ah, much better," came her dad's voice. He rounded the corner into the kitchen, pulled out a chair for Ms. Frank, then seated himself.

Holly couldn't remember Dad pulling out chairs for her mom. She didn't approve.

Setting the rest of the dishes onto the table, Holly took her place and waited while her father said grace. She felt guilty about thanking God for the terrible food they were about to eat, and hoped He understood.

Holly knew she'd have to act as if nothing were wrong or she'd surely get caught. Her dad took several bites before his expression changed from contentment to puzzlement.

She caught a questioning look from him, so she kept her head low, moving the food around on her plate, making it look as though she were eating it.

Dinner was very quiet. Talk seemed forced, not like the animated conversations they had when her mom was around. Ms. Frank kept apologizing for not being very hungry.

Holly felt pleased.

She thought about dessert, wondering what other food she could destroy. Then she remembered Mrs. Kanaga's brownies. Holly served them, but both her victims declined, making her chuckle at the irony. They'd passed up the best part of the whole meal.

Dad and Ms. Frank helped clean the kitchen, then went into the living room. Holly didn't know whether to join them, or be polite and go upstairs. Glancing at the clock, she knew exactly what to do. She clicked on the television.

The three of them watched the end of the news in silence.

Then, on the screen, as if by magic, Jacqueline Mann appeared — in the shower.

Holly tried to look at Dad without turning her head.

His face was purple.

He looked as though he'd swallowed a bar of Chinchilla soap.

"Well!" He leapt to his feet and paced in front of the television, as if that would make the com-

mercial disappear. "It's getting awfully late," he said to the floor.

Ms. Frank looked a bit surprised, but didn't say anything.

In jerky motions, Dad clicked off the TV.

Holly dashed to get their coats, then held open the door, avoiding eye contact. After they left, she retreated to her bedroom, knowing she had about twenty minutes to come up with some good excuses or she'd be grounded until she was ninety.

Twenty minutes later, the front door banged open. "Holly Marie, come down here!"

Holly took her time on the stairs. Was it too late to move to another planet? Alone?

"Hi, Dad." She tried a hug and a grin, but it didn't change her father's disappointed expression.

Holly felt guilty. She hadn't meant to hurt him, just make a bad impression on Ms. Frank.

He slumped on the couch, looking defeated. "Holly, why?" was all he said.

She joined him. "I don't want you to date her."

There. She'd said it.

"Who? Marilyn?" He took a deep breath and leaned back. "Honey, this wasn't a date; it was dinner. That's all."

She wasn't convinced.

"Marilyn and I are just friends. You're the one who introduced us, you know."

Holly remembered. Before summer break, the school had a carnival, and mothers were supposed to bring treats. Since Holly didn't have a mom within a thousand miles of Ketchikan, her dad had taken treats — store-bought, of course. That's when he'd met Ms. Frank.

Dad took her hands in his. "I thought it might be good for you to have a woman around every once in a while, instead of just me all the time."

"I have women around all day — teachers."

He acted as if that had never occurred to him. "You're absolutely right. Ignore my good intentions."

He brushed hair from her forehead. "Holly, I want you to know I love your mother very much. I'm not looking for anyone to take her place."

Holly's throat tightened as she watched Dad's eyes turn misty. She hugged him.

He sniffed a little. "At least I still have you."

Pulling away, Dad regained his composure. "Now let's talk about dinner."

"I was hoping you'd forget."

"Did you do it on purpose?"

"Wel-l-l-l, it began as an accident, then I sort of helped it along. I really didn't mean to shipwreck the casserole."

He laughed. "But once you did, you thought it'd be fine to go ahead and serve plane-crash potatoes."

Holly joined his laughter. "And train-derailment salad."

"Automobile-accident rolls."

"Capsized gravy."

Her dad wiped his eyes from half-crying and half-laughing. "What catastrophe befell the brownies that I'm not even aware of? Are they bicycle-blowout brownies?"

"No, the brownies are perfect. Mrs. Kanaga made them. I'll give the pan to Beth; she'll eat them." Holly started to rise, but her dad pulled her back to the couch.

"You'll give those perfect brownies to Beth over my dead body."

Holly prepared a plate of brownies for the two of them to share. A warm feeling surrounded her like a California morning.

In the same day, both Mom and Dad had confided to her that they still loved each other.

Now the rest was all up to her.

10

The liver pâté worked. Gary had been right; it was much easier to use, melting into the cookies without a trace.

But there were problems. First, the same amount of money it took to buy a pound of chicken livers only netted them two ounces of pâté. They'd go broke.

And second, the pâté was pumped full of fat and chemicals. Using it went against everything healthy HJ's stood for.

There was no choice. They were doomed to chop slimy liver for as long as they made the cookies.

Holly swallowed the last bite of a test cookie, then opened her notebook on the Tiptons' kitchen table and wrote the final instructions for the recipe: *Bake at 350 degrees for twelve to fifteen minutes.*

"Ta-da!" She held up both hands in a victory gesture while Beth cheered.

"Now let's hear plan B," Beth said. "The plan

we have to resort to since we can't set up HJ's on Front Street." She gave Holly a challenging look. "You haven't come up with a plan B yet, have you?"

"Yes, as a matter of fact, I have," Holly replied, glancing at the clock. Today's experiment had taken so long, she guessed her dad was home by now, and she wasn't there to greet him, nor had she left a note.

But surely he could figure out where she was, and not ground her.

She nibbled another cookie. They were slightly addictive in spite of the liver. Maybe she should take some home for her dad to explain why she was late. She'd been baking something special — just for him. He'd be pleased.

"I have good news and bad news," Holly continued. "Mrs. Molesworth checked with the principal. She gave us permission to set up HJ's in the school cafeteria."

"You're kidding!" Beth exclaimed. "Mrs. Annett said yes?"

Holly nodded. "Providing we charge a reasonable amount for our product. So I told her each item on our menu would sell for twenty-five cents."

"Only twenty-five cents?" Beth grimaced. "Is that the bad news?"

"Nope, here's the bad news. Both of them — Mrs. Molesworth and Mrs. Annett — want to sample our products before we set up the stand."

"So? These taste fine."

"They *taste* fine, but what are we going to *call* them? Do you really think if we put up a sign that says LIVER COOKIES FOR SALE, kids will rush to plunk down their quarters? No one is going to eat a Liver cookie on purpose."

"We have to call them something else."

"Brilliant, Eliza," said Gary, who'd been listening from the other room. He joined Holly at the table.

They all reached for cookies, munching while they considered the problem. "I got it," Holly said. She broke a cookie apart and arranged it on the table.

"What is that supposed to be?"

"An L," she replied. "Since we shortened Healthy Junk Snacks to HJ's, we can shorten Liver cookies to L cookies."

Brian came through the front door with a great deal of noise, yelled upstairs to his mom, then wandered into the kitchen, listening to their discussion about L cookies.

"Elk cookies?" he broke in. "Now you're going to bake cookies with elk meat?" He looked nauseated from the mere thought of it.

"No," Beth answered, swatting at him. "Holly's using an acronym."

Holly's pencil lead snapped. "I'm using a what?"

"Acronym. It's when you call something by its

initials instead of its name. Like IBM, FBI, or in this case, L cookies."

Holly filed the word in her memory, rushing on before it got late enough for Dad to call the Missing Persons Bureau. "Broccoli cola will now be called B cola — and we'd better get busy fast on the other recipes."

"Why?" Brian asked. "Are you afraid someone's going to steal your stupid idea? I wouldn't worry about it; it's too repulsive."

"No." Holly wished Brian would leave them alone. "I didn't finish telling you the bad news part. Mrs. Annett and Mrs. Molesworth want to sample all our products — on Friday."

"Friday! That's day after tomorrow."

"Brilliant, Eliza," Gary said.

"Who's Eliza?" Brian looked from one girl to the other.

Beth consoled herself with another cookie as Holly continued, "We've got forty-eight hours to come up with some more repul — " She stopped, frowning at Brian for putting the word into her head. "Some more *recipes* for HJ's."

"Let's brainstorm," Gary said, pulling a pen from his pocket and sliding Holly's notebook in front of him.

Her heart stopped.

She'd scribbled Gary's name all over the next page. What if he could read it through the top sheet? Or what if he turned the page?

Oblivious to the stopping of her heart, Gary said, "How did you come up with the idea for Liver — excuse me — L cookies in the first place?"

"We took a poll," Holly answered, a bit breathy from lack of heartbeats. "Here are the questions." She grabbed her notebook, slid it back to safety, then flipped to a page in the middle, burying her telltale scribbles.

Her heart began to beat once more. "Tell me the junk food you love the most."

He grinned. "Pudding."

"Now tell me the healthy food you hate the worst."

He thought a moment. "Peas."

"Great," Holly said. "Our next recipe will be pea pudding, or as an *acronym*," she added, giving a sidelong glance to Beth, "P pudding."

Holly stopped. "Wait, that doesn't work. Pea pudding is still P pudding."

Brian snickered. "Either way, it sounds sickening."

She turned to Gary again. "What's your *second* unfavorite healthy food?"

"Spinach."

"Great, that works." She erased the P and wrote S. "S pudding for Spinach pudding. Perfect."

"I didn't think anyone could turn me off in the food department," Brian said flamboyantly, as if he were acting in one of his plays. "But I feel more like doing my homework than eating right now, and I never — "

"Brian," Holly interrupted. "We don't have much time. What's *your* favorite junk food?"

"Ummmm." He leaned against the refrigerator, locking his hands behind his head. "Milk shakes. Any flavor."

"And the healthy food you hate?"

"That's easy. Tuna."

"Voilà," Holly exclaimed. "We now offer Tuna shakes, also known as T shakes."

"I am *not* going to be a part of this." Brian headed for the door. "You children are crazy if you think you can survive in the business world offering such terrible products."

"Wait until you try our T shake," Gary said, sounding like a commercial announcer. "Coming soon to a stomach near you!"

"I'll *never* try your T shake," Brian said. "Besides, *girls* can't start a business on their own. They just don't have what it takes." He tapped the side of his head, where, Holly assumed, his brain was supposed to be.

"Lucky for you girls you've got Gary's help," he added with a smirk.

Holly's temperature rose with his words. She vowed to make the T shake so good, even Brian would love it.

"We need one more recipe," Beth said. Brian's

comments hadn't bothered her at all.

"Why?" Gary asked.

"Five is a good round number."

"Five is an odd number," he reminded her.

"Okay, we need *two* more recipes. Who can we poll?"

Holly grabbed her raincoat. "Ask your mom the love/hate questions, and I'll run home and ask my dad — and warn him we'll be working late tonight and tomorrow night."

She grabbed a few L cookies and threw them into a paper bag, holding them up as she ran for the door.

"Peace offering for being late," she explained. "I hope it works."

11

Friday morning, Holly and Beth tore Mrs. Tipton away from chapter eleven of her newest novel to drive them to school. They'd overslept after staying up half the night creating and baking snacks for HJ's.

Both were glad they'd missed the school bus, since they doubted their snacks would survive the trip. Hiding treats from kids on the bus was impossible.

Any kind of treats.

While Holly and Beth waited in the cafeteria for Mrs. Molesworth and Mrs. Annett, they arranged the snacks in an appealing manner. Everything looked and smelled as normal as a church bake sale — especially the results of their last two love/hate polls.

From Holly's dad had come Tomato pie, but since they'd already used a T for T shake, they decided to call it *quick* tomato pie, or QT pie. From

Beth's mom had come Okra fudge, also known as O fudge.

The teacher and principal arrived, donned their eyeglasses in unison, then studied the snacks as if they expected one of them to move. Holly arranged a sample of each treat on a plate while Beth served.

Mrs. Annett and Mrs. Molesworth acted like judges at a county fair, *oohing* and *ahhing* after each mouthful.

Holly held her breath.

Beth crossed her fingers behind her back.

"Marvelous!" exclaimed Mrs. Annett.

"Delicious!" exclaimed Mrs. Molesworth. She took another swallow of B cola, then nodded her approval.

"Girls," Mrs. Annett said, "you have our permission to set up your snack stand for one month here in the school cafeteria."

Holly held the cafeteria door open while Gary maneuvered through, carrying a large cardboard box filled with paper plates and napkins, all donated to their project by the PTA. In return, the three partners had agreed to donate ten percent of their sales to one of the PTA's causes.

Holly didn't mind being generous with her profit, but now it would take longer to save for a plane ticket to California.

Being in the school building on a Saturday

morning with no one around gave Holly an eerie feeling, but Mrs. Annett had told them it would be the best time to build their snack stand.

Beth was at the orthodontist's, so it was Holly and Gary doing all the work, which didn't bother Holly one bit.

The sun was shining for a change, and it matched Holly's mood. She felt like going to the beach, but there wasn't one. Here in Ketchikan, the beach was more like a rocky cliff.

The school janitor had delivered a carnival booth from the storage closet, along with some cleaning supplies. The booth was a bit dilapidated, but Holly thought she could clean and repair it.

Gary helped her scoot the booth against one wall. "Mrs. Molesworth left the door to her classroom unlocked so we could get to the art supplies."

He pointed at the dusty booth. "You clean while I round up some paint and paper."

Holly threw a sponge at him. "You sound like Brian. Why don't *you* clean while *I* collect the art supplies?"

Gary looked startled by the flying sponge as well as her words. "Sure, I guess so." He headed toward a drinking fountain to get some water.

She felt embarrassed about snapping at him. "What's your favorite color?" she asked in a softer voice.

"Why?"

"We'll paint the snack stand our favorite colors. Mine is orange, yours is — "

"Blue."

"And Beth's is . . . what *is* Beth's favorite color? I should know; I'm her best friend."

"Last time I asked," Gary answered, squeezing water from the sponge, "she said beryl."

"Beryl?"

Gary began to scrub, offering no explanation, so Holly slipped from the cafeteria, leaving her shoe jammed between the double doors to keep them from locking behind her.

She followed a darkened hallway to Mrs. Molesworth's classroom, then gathered a long strip of white paper for a banner, plus paintbrushes, scrap paper, and orange and blue paint.

Holly sorted through the remaining paint pots, knowing she was wasting her time. None of them were labeled *beryl*.

Borrowing the dictionary from Mrs. Molesworth's desk, she looked up the word. Beryl wasn't a color at all. It was a mineral — but it must be a shade of green since emeralds and aquamarines come from it.

Holly gritted her teeth. Why couldn't Beth simply say her favorite color was *green*?

"What's taking you so long?"

Holly jumped at Gary's voice. She slammed the dictionary shut, and headed back to the art supply cabinet.

"The booth is clean, and now I have dishpan hands." Gary held out his palms. "Does this make me a geek? Is Brian right?"

She smiled at his comment, grabbed a jar of basic green paint, and followed him back to the cafeteria.

Holly retrieved her shoe from the doorway, then helped Gary spread the banner onto a table. Opening paint pots, she watched him letter the word *menu*.

Holly wondered if Gary liked her.

Well, she knew he liked her, but did he *like* her? As much as she liked him?

Dipping a brush in orange paint, she drew the H in *HJ's*.

"So," she began, watching him from the corner of her eye, "your favorite color is blue, and your favorite food is pudding. What's your favorite . . . season?"

"Fall."

"What's your favorite sport?"

"Football."

Holly traced outside the orange letters with blue. Gary's color surrounding her color. It made her feel warm inside.

She cleared her throat. "Who's your favorite . . . person?" Her voice wavered over the word *person*.

"It's — "

"Or, just their initials," she blurted, too nervous

to hear what he might say. "If you'd rather."

Gary looked puzzled. "The initials are — " He squinted toward the ceiling, thinking. "H.M."

Holly gasped, putting an extra squiggle in the S in cookies. He *did* like her! H.M. for Holly Mann.

She felt hot and cold at the same time, as if half of her were buried in an Alaskan snowbank, and half were on a California beach.

The entire English language disappeared from her memory. Silence expanded in the room like a rising balloon.

"And you?" Gary's words made her jump.

"And me, what?" Did he want her to say she liked him back?

"You answer the questions you just asked me."

Holly gulped. "Favorite food, quiche."

"Season?"

Should she say *fall* so he'd think they had a lot in common, or should she tell the truth? She voted on the truth. "Summer."

"Sport?"

"Softball." She liked softball because she'd played second base on a team in California.

"Favorite person?"

She wanted to say, *"You, Gary, can't you tell?"*

Instead, she played his game and said, "G.T."

"G.T." He scratched his chin, smearing green paint across it like a pointy beard. "I don't know who that is."

How could he be so dense?

The silence ballooned bigger.

"I can't figure it out," he said. "I'll tell you who my initials stand for if you tell me. It's really no big deal."

Holly couldn't hold her hand steady enough to paint. *No big deal*, he'd said.

"Okay," she answered. "But you have to go first."

"Sure. H.M. is Houston Maddock."

"Who?" Holly tipped a paint pot. Orange paint spread in a circle like a bright sun at the top of the banner.

"Houston Maddock. He plays tight end for Ketchikan High." Gary's eyes grew dreamy. "He's fantastic."

Holly spelled pudding with three d's and had to start over.

"And who's G.T.?" Gary asked.

"It's — " Holly didn't know anyone on the Ketchikan High football team. She thought fast. "It's an old *boyfriend*," she explained, watching for Gary's reaction. "Gilbert Titus."

Holly felt pleased she'd connected the initials with a real person back in Los Angeles. Only Gilbert Titus wore long hair, dirty jeans, no socks, and would never qualify as boyfriend material.

No reaction from Gary. He held up his side of the banner. "Let's tape this across the top of the booth before my mom honks for us."

Holly added a few quick strokes, making the orange sun look like it was supposed to be there. She stepped on a chair and taped her side of the banner while Gary taped his side.

HJ's SNACK STAND it read in orange, blue, and beryl letters, somewhat squiggly.

Then:

MENU

25 Cents Each

| L COOKIES | B COLA | S PUDDING |
| T SHAKES | QT PIE | O FUDGE |

Holly and Gary studied their accomplishment.

"It needs one more thing." Gary scribbled on another paper. "Grand opening on Monday," he read out loud as he printed the words.

Holly taped up the sign, then shook hands with Gary.

"Congratulations, partner," he said, grinning at her with his beryl beard.

"Congratulations," she returned, shaking his hand once more.

Maybe she couldn't compete with Houston Maddock for the honor of being Gary's favorite person, but being his partner in business was almost as nice.

12

Holly leaned her elbows on top of a wood railing as she watched a floatplane land on the watery runway of the channel separating Ketchikan from Gravina Island.

Water sprayed in giant arcs as the plane touched down. The pilot was bringing tourists back from their flightseeing trip to the Misty Fiords.

Holly was waiting outside the Pioneer Pantry for her dad to pay for breakfast. Weekends were their times to spend together playing tourist, but for the last month, Holly had been wrapped up in HJ's morning, noon, and night, seven days a week.

She smiled at a strolling couple as she thought about the success of HJ's. What a hit the healthy junk snacks had been, yet none of the kids at school knew they were getting good health along with the junk.

And the money was coming in, although not as much or as fast as Holly had hoped. Mrs. Annett had limited orders to two selections to prevent students from skipping lunch and eating only snacks.

The stand was averaging sales of $25 a day. Holly had already calculated her first month's take. After deducting ten percent for the PTA, $10 a day to cover supplies, then splitting what was left three ways, she'd only made about $130 — a long way from the $500 she needed for round-trip plane fare to Los Angeles.

Maybe she could shoot for half the amount — just enough to get to L.A. She'd worry about flying back to Ketchikan later.

Her dad appeared, zipping his heavy jacket. "Ready?" he asked, taking her arm. It was a bit cold to be strolling down Front Street in November, but Holly felt guilty about never spending time with her father anymore.

She tried not to think about Gary and Beth at home, doubling up on baking chores this morning because of her absence. Saturdays and Sundays were now spent stockpiling snacks to sell during the week, then taking them to school to store in the cafeteria's huge walk-in refrigerator.

"It's nice to see my daughter in broad daylight," Dad teased. "I'd forgotten what you look like." He stepped back to give her the once-over. "I think you've grown a couple of inches since I saw you last."

"Da-ad." Holly's guilt level was already overflowing. She didn't need any more piled on.

"What shall we do today?" he asked, pulling a visitors' guide from his jacket pocket. "We can browse through the Tongass Historical Museum, see the Raven-Stealing-the-Sun totem pole, visit the Deer Mountain Fish Hatchery, shop on Creek Street — "

"That's it," Holly interrupted. "I want to shop on Creek Street because I'm tired of walking around in squishy wet tennis shoes every day."

"You got it."

Holly took Dad's hand and pulled him up a wooden sidewalk bordering the icy creek that gave the street its name. She stepped into the first shoe shop they found, and bought a pair of leather boots with rubber soles. The salesperson called them Alaskan sneakers.

Holly showed her dad the pair of beaded Tlingit Indian moccasins she'd been dying to own ever since they moved to Ketchikan. She hoped he got the hint, since Christmas was around the corner.

Glancing at her watch, she felt a tug to get home and help her partners bake. She also felt a tug to catch up on her homework. Being an entrepreneur was certainly a lot more work than she'd realized.

"Now what?" her dad asked, studying the visitors' guide again. "Shall we go see the world's largest gold nugget?"

"Dad." Holly yanked at his sleeve. "I really need to get home."

"Home?"

She could read the disappointment in his eyes. "I'm sorry," she said. "I've got so much to do anymore."

He folded the visitors' guide without emotion, then shoved it into his pocket. "Isn't it about time you gave up HJ's?"

"Gave it up?"

He started down Creek Street at a brisk pace. "I thought it was a Social Studies assignment, not a lifelong career."

"Well, it was, but it's become so successful." Holly looped her arm through his as they walked. "Don't you want your daughter to be successful?" She leaned in front of him and raised her eyebrows a couple of times, giving him a silly look.

But he didn't return her amusement. A somber expression she couldn't read shadowed his face, and he didn't answer.

"Well, *don't* you?" she persisted.

Dad stopped abruptly, wrapping his arms around her in a hug. "Yes, Holly, I'm very proud of you." His voice was muffled. "But why does success have to take you away from me?"

Holly returned the hug, ignoring stares from

78

passersby. The meaning behind his words suddenly became as crystal clear to her as the ice-cold water rippling down the creek beside them. Success had taken Mom away from him, and now it was taking her away.

Dad's words from the night Ms. Frank came to dinner flashed through her mind. *"At least I still have you,"* he'd said. But for the last month, he hadn't had her at all — her time, or her attention.

"Well." Dad pulled away and smoothed her hair. "Let's get you home, then." His voice was light, but sadness still clouded his eyes.

Throwing back his head, he addressed the gray-black sky, which was starting to spit snow at them. "What are we doing out in this terrible weather, anyway? I'm freezing."

He hurried her toward the car. "This is a good day for staying in and baking those strange-tasting cookies you insist on making."

Holly laughed. She'd never let her dad in on the secret ingredient her cookies contained.

Her smile soon disappeared as thoughts of Mom returned. Suddenly she could see why Mom had been so determined to stay in California in spite of Dad's disapproval.

Mom's busy career had come between her parents, and now Holly was following in her mother's footsteps.

What was she supposed to do? Could she give up HJ's for her dad? Was it fair of him to ask her to?

Holly felt as if a clamp had been loosened from her heart as she realized the impossible choice Mom had been forced to make before they moved to Alaska.

Climbing into the car, she stared out the window. All of a sudden she didn't feel quite so angry at her mother anymore.

13

"Hey, Cheechako!" Brian called from his mom's car as he and Mrs. Tipton sped past Holly on her way home from the bus stop. "I saw your mother in the shower last night!"

Holly cringed as kids around her on the street laughed.

They all knew what Brian meant. When she first moved here, Holly had opened her big mouth and bragged about Mom filming television commercials. Now she was sorry she'd told anyone. Her words were coming back to haunt her.

She'd taped all Mom's commercials except the one in the shower. She'd never even watched it all the way to the end.

Running up the steps, Holly unlocked the door, made her mandatory phone call to Dad's office, then sifted through the mail. A postcard bordered with Hollywood palm trees caught her eye:

Dear Holly Marie,

Miss you!
Am not sending a list of air times
for my newest commercials since there
aren't any. Work is slow because all
holidays ads were filmed last June us-
ing fake snow.

Now agencies are booking suntan
lotion commercials for bikini-clad
models. Unfortunately, the sponsors
want teenagers inside the bikinis, not
somebody's mother who's on the wrong
side of thirty.

Gotta go to another audition —
this time for a computer ad. (Boring.)
But Sam (the Chinchilla soap man) is
auditioning, too, so it should be fun.

> *Kisses and Hugs,*
> *Mom*

Holly let her jacket slide to the floor. The postcard had thrilled her — until she'd gotten to the
last line. Thank heavens her mom would be wearing a business suit instead of a bikini if she filmed
an ad for computers. But did the soap man have
to be part of it?

"Holly, are you all right?" came a voice from
the kitchen.

She jumped. "Mrs. Kanaga! I forgot you were here today."

As Holly moved toward the kitchen, the possibility of not being with her mother for Christmas tumbled down on her heart. It seemed like a million years had passed since last Christmas back in Los Angeles.

Mrs. Kanaga gave her a tender look, then held out her arms and scooped Holly inside.

Tears blurred Holly's eyes as Mrs. Kanaga "tsk-tsked" into her ear.

"What's wrong, child?"

"Nothing."

Holly stepped back, sniffling and shrugging. "I mean, *everything*."

She prided herself on acting as if nothing were wrong, like a grown-up. But the last month had been hard.

Thanksgiving dinner had been more like a funeral than a holiday. Both she and her dad were lost in their own private memories of past Thanksgivings, even though Mrs. Kanaga had surprised them the night before by bringing over a turkey with potatoes, gravy, and cranberry sauce.

If they hadn't been invited to the Tiptons' house for dessert, Holly would have been even more depressed. The only fun part of the whole day was when she and Beth invented a recipe for turkey éclairs.

Mrs. Kanaga let Holly hold on to her and cry, not prying into her problems.

"Taste your tears," she whispered in a soothing voice, "and if they're salty, you're crying for no good reason."

Holly knew she was crying for a lot of no good reasons, but Mrs. Kanaga's words made her feel better. She still didn't have enough money for the flight to California, Mom was excited about the soap man again, and her dad had been talking on the phone a lot lately. Holly didn't know whether it was to Ms. Frank or to someone new.

Feeling angry at herself for crying like a first-grader, she was glad Dad wasn't here. She'd been trying so hard to convince him she could take care of herself, and didn't need to call him every afternoon at three-thirty on the dot for fear he'd round up a posse to track her down.

Reluctantly she pulled away from Mrs. Kanaga, giving her a kiss on one plump cheek. "Thanks," was all she needed to say. Somehow she knew Mrs. Kanaga, who'd raised twelve children of her own, understood.

Holly ran upstairs and splashed water on her face until it wasn't obvious she'd been crying. Then she changed into comfortable gray sweats, grabbed an umbrella, and dashed through the rain to Beth's house.

Mrs. Molesworth and Mrs. Annett had asked them to continue HJ's for the rest of the semester because of its unexpected popularity with both kids and teachers. So the three partners had decided to create one new healthy junk snack in honor of the holiday season.

The Tiptons' door was cracked open. Holly let herself inside.

"We're in the kitchen!" Gary called.

Throwing her coat over a chair, Holly turned and collided with Mrs. Tipton. There was no doubt she was the mother of Beth, Brian, and Gary. The similarity in looks always struck Holly whenever she saw her.

"Aren't you working on your novel today?" Holly asked.

"It's finished!" Mrs. T cried, wildly flinging a scarf around her neck. Holly could easily see where Brian inherited his flair for dramatics.

Mrs. Tipton dove into the closet, sorting through coats. "May I borrow your down jacket, Lizzie?"

"Don't call me Lizzie!" came Beth's angry voice from the kitchen.

Mrs. Tipton backed out of the closet and winked at Holly. "She'll tell you all about it."

"I already know. I was in class when it happened," Holly whispered, trying not to laugh at her best friend's misfortune.

"May I borrow your down jacket, Elizabeth Karen Tipton?"

"Yes, Mom!" Beth called back in a much sweeter voice.

Mrs. Tipton grabbed her purse and keys. "After I finish writing a book, I have to stop being an author, and turn back into a mother for a few weeks until I get to know my family again."

She gave Holly a hug, then whispered into her ear. "And go Christmas shopping — what does my daughter want? Did she tell you?"

"Same thing I want," Holly whispered back, wishing her own mom would borrow *her* jacket and go Christmas shopping for *their* family. "Tlingit Indian moccasins."

"That's right, I remember the hints you two kept dropping at Thanksgiving. Thanks, kid. It's nice having you around."

"Bye," Holly said, watching her leave. Why couldn't she resemble her own mom as much as Beth resembled Mrs. Tipton?

"Hol-lee!"

Rushing into the kitchen, she found herself in the middle of a sibling war.

"We're using the love/hate question to come up with a new holiday snack for HJ's, right?" Beth asked.

"Right," Holly agreed.

"And Gary — "

"Stupendous guy that he is," Gary interjected.

"*Stupid* guy that he is," Beth corrected, waving

a spoon at him, "insists on using *fruit* as the healthy food, and *cake* as the junk food."

"So?" Holly didn't see anything wrong with that.

"It's been done. Haven't you ever heard of *fruitcake*?"

"But" — Gary waved a spoon back at her — "regular fruitcake has those yucky mystery fruits in it. We would use *real* fruit."

"That's been done, too." Beth acted as if Gary were trying to reinvent the basic peanut butter-and-jelly sandwich. "Haven't you ever heard of apple cake, banana bread, or pineapple upside-down cake?"

"But the fruit is all mushed up. I'm talking about big slices of fruit in the cake, Lizzie."

Beth threw the wooden spoon at him. "Don't call me Lizzie! I'll decide when to change my name and what to change it to. And I'm not changing it just because we read some stupid story in school about a maniac girl who chopped up her parents with an ax."

Holly knew if she looked at Gary she'd burst out laughing, and that's exactly what happened. She and Gary howled while Beth stormed around the kitchen, now waving a spatula.

This morning, after reading class had finished the story of Lizzie Borden, Mrs. Molesworth taught them the song:

Lizzie Borden took an ax
Gave her mother forty whacks.
When she saw what she had done,
She gave her father forty-one.

For the rest of the day, everyone in class had called Beth *Lizzie.* Holly had never seen her friend so furious.

Holly tried to stop laughing, but every time she looked at Gary, she started in again.

"Stop!" Beth demanded, stomping her foot. "It's not funny, Holly,"

"That's not Holly," Gary answered for her. "It's . . . it's Hollandaise. Hollandaise Mann!"

Holly slid from her chair in hysterics.

"Gary!" screamed his sister.

"That's not Gary," Holly said between gulps of air. "That's . . . that's Garlic! Garlic Tipton."

Gary slumped to the floor, too. "And you can't call us Holly and Gary anymore; you have to call us Hollandaise and Garlic. We won't answer to anything else."

Beth turned her back, but Holly saw her hiding a smile. She finally gave in to their teasing and joined the laughter.

"You guys are mean!" she scolded. "Okay, you win. I'm Beth, and I'm going to stay Beth."

"I never thought I'd hear you say that — Elizabeth."

"It's Beth!"

Holly wiped away her laughing tears. "Could we get back to our other argument before I have to go home? The fruitcake fight?"

They were all quiet for a moment, regaining their collective composure and planning their holiday recipe.

"If we use an unusual fruit, it might work," said Beth.

"Name some fruits," Gary suggested, then began, "Cantaloupe cake, orange cake, pear cake, grape cake."

"Not unusual enough," Beth said.

"Okay." He tried again, flipping through a cookbook in reference. "How about mango cake, kiwi cake, guava cake, kumquat cake?"

"Too unusual. I don't know what any of those fruits look like. How can I shop for them?"

"I got it." Holly snapped her fingers. "Bring me a dictionary."

"Dictionary cake?" Gary raised an eyebrow at her, then ran upstairs to borrow one off his mom's desk.

Holly grabbed the dictionary from Gary as soon as he returned. She thumbed through the pages. "Ah-ha. I'm right. Our Christmas fruitcake will be made with an unusual fruit after all — avocado! And it's green, too, for Christmas!"

She grinned at her friends as the idea sunk in. "Avocado cake."

Holly held up an empty dish and faced her audience. "Introducing our new, improved fruit-cake, with a secret ingredient."

She cocked her head toward an invisible TV camera.

"Fruitcake — it's not just for Christmas any-more!"

14

Holly held out her hand until the fourth-grader before her plopped two quarters into her palm. Then she dished up a generous helping of S pudding with a slice of fruitcake on the side. Not real fruitcake, of course, but wheat-and-honey cake filled with chunks of avocados.

She glanced at the clock, then at the long line snaking around the cafeteria table in front of HJ's. Gary should be here any minute to take over.

The three partners rotated shifts, each taking a lunch break with a different grade level. Holly had eaten her lunch in between waiting on third- and fourth-graders, who were now heading back to class. Gary would serve the fifth- and sixth-graders while eating his own lunch in bits and pieces, and Beth had already served the first-and second-graders.

Catching Ms. Frank's eye as the teacher returned her empty lunch tray, Holly waved, glad that she and Ms. Frank were still friends after her disaster dinner, as it had come to be called.

A hand tapped her shoulder, making her jump. Gary had slipped through the back of the booth. Holly moved out of the way as he stepped into her place, smooth as green bean icing.

"We're doing great today," she whispered. "I can hardly lift the cash box, it's so heavy with change."

Gary was too busy to answer, so Holly left.

She hurried to math class, where she spent the hour figuring out her finances instead of working the problems Mrs. Molesworth had written on the board.

It was two weeks until winter break. Holly had managed to save $225, and since sales had been up the last couple of weeks, she felt sure she could easily collect the additional $25 in two weeks.

She'd finally have enough money for a plane ticket to Los Angeles.

But not back.

It was hard to breathe, just thinking about going home for Christmas. But something was keeping her from feeling totally happy about it.

Dad.

How could she enjoy Christmas in California without him? Yet, how could she enjoy Christmas in Alaska without Mom?

It wasn't fair she should have to choose.

Holly wondered when to tell Dad about her

plans for the holidays. She couldn't just disappear. What would he say?

Suddenly she felt sick. She shouldn't have eaten so much QT pie today at HJ's. How could she leave her dad alone for Christmas?

Would he think she was deserting him like Mom had? Would he think she loved Mom more than she loved him?

Her great idea was becoming more complicated than she'd planned. If she stayed here, she'd have at least $225 to spend on Christmas presents — $225 would buy a *lot* of presents. And Mom could spend Christmas with the soap man, which she probably wanted to do anyway.

"Holly Mann, I'm speaking to you." Mrs. Molesworth's voice exploded into her daydream. "What is the answer to number nine?"

"Two hundred twenty-five," Holly blurted, not even knowing the question.

The class laughed.

"Holly, that's not even close," Mrs. Molesworth said. "See me after school."

By the time Holly convinced Mrs. Molesworth she could solve the unknown x factor, the school bus had left. Now she'd have to walk home in the freezing drizzle and be late for her phone call to Dad.

Plus, the school counselor had given her a series

of leaflets called *What It's Like When Your Parents Get Divorced*, and had made her promise to read them. Holly wanted to trash the leaflets, but the counselor had waited until she'd tucked them into her book bag.

As she walked home, Mrs. Tipton's car pulled up, and a familiar face stuck his head out the back window. "Need a ride, Cheechako?"

Grateful for a warm, dry ride, Holly hopped into the front seat with Mrs. Tipton because a girl was sitting in back with Brian.

There was room for about three more people in the backseat because the girl was almost sitting on Brian's lap. She was wearing enough makeup for about three people, too, Holly noticed.

She faced forward, trying not to stare.

"This little twirp," Brian said to his girlfriend, "is my neighbor."

"She's not a little twirp," the girl replied.

Holly liked her instantly.

"You're right," Brian agreed. "She's a *smart* little twirp."

"Yeah?"

"Yeah. She and my sister — another smart little twirp — started their own business."

"Yeah?"

"Yeah. They opened a restaurant."

"Bri-yan, it's not a restaurant." Holly felt self-conscious. Brian was actually bragging about her and Beth. "It's only a snack stand."

"Yeah?" The girl leaned forward to get a better look at Holly.

Is *yeah* the only word she knew?

"Yeah, they're making big bucks."

"No, we're not, Brian."

"How much have you made?"

"The three of us together?"

He nodded.

"Almost nine hundred dollars."

"Yeah?" Brian, the girl, and Mrs. Tipton said together.

"Yeah," Holly replied, feeling proud. She had a right to be proud. She'd gotten an A on her Social Studies project, and now had extra money in her pocket.

It *was* pretty impressive.

Brian's mom eased the car in between two others in front of their house. Holly stepped out. "Thanks for the ride, Mrs. T." She waved to her. "And nice to meet you," she said to the *yeah* girl.

The girl smiled at Holly. "I'm very impressed," she said. "Keep up the hard work, and you might own a whole chain of restaurants someday."

"That's the spirit," Mrs. Tipton threw in.

Holly felt herself blush. Maybe she *would* own a whole chain of HJ's someday — all across Alaska. Or, all across the whole country. Why not?

She held her book bag over her head to block the rain, then bounded up the cement steps. Turning the key in the door, she heard the phone ring.

Holly rushed in, dropped her books, and lunged for the speaker button. "Hello?" she gasped.

"Is this the Mann of the house?"

"Hello, Dad."

"You're late."

"Da-ad." He was never going to change. "I missed the bus because I had to stay after school, so Beth's mom drove me home."

"It's okay," he said. "I called with special news."

"Yeah?" Holly said, sounding like Brian's girlfriend.

The other end of the line fell silent. It sounded as if Dad were pacing.

Oh, no. "What is it, Dad?" Would she have to stage another disaster dinner?

He cleared his throat. "We're having company for Christmas."

Holly sank to the couch. *There goes my trip to California.*

She could think of nothing more depressing than spending Christmas with her dad and a stranger. "Is it the person you've been talking to on the phone lately?"

"Yes."

Her heart sagged as if it were overflowing with Ketchikan rain. Christmas was going to be awful this year. Worse than Thanksgiving. "That's the person who's spending Christmas with us?"

"Yes!" Her dad's enthusiasm only made it worse. "Holly Marie, I thought you'd be thrilled." Now he sounded hurt.

Holly couldn't stop the tears. "How can I be thrilled about spending Christmas with somebody I don't even know?" Her voice had risen with each word until it squeaked. Holly punched the speaker button, shutting off the phone. She wasn't going to sit there crying and squeaking in her dad's ear.

Ringgggggg!

Holly knew it was Dad calling back, so she let it ring a couple of times before picking up the receiver.

"Hello," she said in a trembly voice.

"Are you crying because your mother is coming here for Christmas?"

Holly stopped breathing. "Mom? Mom is coming *here*?"

"That's what I've been trying to tell you."

"I thought you said it was the person you've been calling — "

As soon as the words were out of her mouth, she realized all those late-night phone calls had been to her very own mom.

"Doesn't a man have a right to call his wife on the telephone?"

"Dad! That's fantastic! I can't wait!"

"Well, that's the reaction I was hoping to hear."

Holly said good-bye, then snatched the leaflets

on having divorced parents from her book bag and flung them into the air.

As they fluttered around her like giant snow-flakes, Holly shouted, "Mom is coming to Alaska for Christmas!"

15

Holly's heart was doing flip-flops as she watched the Alaska Airlines jet touch down on the runway in the late-morning mist. She glanced at her dad. His heart must be doing flip-flops, too, because he kept pacing from the ticket counter to the water fountain and back again.

It seemed like an eternity before Mom's face appeared among the crowd of passengers. "Mom!" Holly cried, waving a closed umbrella above her head. "Over here!"

Mom's look of anxiety melted into a smile as their eyes met. The crowd was predictably heavy for Christmas Eve, but Holly waded through, reaching out toward Mom for a hug.

Mom seemed shorter, but smelled familiar, like Vanderbilt, her favorite perfume.

"Holly, you've gotten taller!" Mom exclaimed, cupping Holly's face and kissing both cheeks. Mom looked gorgeous in a full-length green coat, with hat, gloves, and scarf coordinated to match.

She stepped back to look Holly over, then rubbed both her daughter's cheeks, which, Holly assumed, were smeared with lipstick. "Happy birthday, dear." Mom hugged her again, then pulled a small gift from her pocket. Her mom always separated birthday gifts from Christmas presents, since the two holidays were so close.

"Thank you," Holly said. She watched Mom's eyes travel over the crowd, looking a bit worried.

"Didn't your father — ?" She stopped as she spotted him.

Holly followed her gaze. Dad was still by the water fountain, looking lost and forgotten.

She froze as her parents moved toward each other. The crowd parted for them, as if they knew something special was about to happen.

Holly pretended she was looking through a television camera, filming a Kodak homecoming commercial.

She'd never seen her dad act shy before. She wanted him to catch Mom up in his arms and swing her around, as he did his own daughter every day when he got home from work.

Instead, her parents simply stared at each other, as if they were meeting for the first time on a blind date. Holly turned her imaginary camera away for a moment, embarrassed.

A second later she looked back, unable to watch, yet unable not to watch. Her dad pulled a small bouquet of yellow roses from inside his rain parka.

Mom acted surprised, then touched her heart like a young girl. Holly knew how much she loved yellow roses.

All of a sudden Mom was crying and hugging Dad. Holly started crying as well, just watching them. Strangers in the airport stared.

Dad motioned toward Holly, so she joined them, hugging and crying, too. She didn't care what anyone else thought. Her family was complete again.

Conversation during the car trip home was reserved and polite. Holly shared the front seat with her parents, sitting in the middle. Mom *oohed* and *ahhed* at all they pointed out to her, but kept commenting on the icy sleet slamming against the car as they drove.

Holly had hoped the weather would cooperate today, but it hadn't. She knew Mom wouldn't like the weather here. Not after sunny California.

"We're going to have a white Christmas," Holly said, trying to change Mom's attitude about cold weather. "You'd never have a white Christmas back in Los Angeles."

Mom laughed at Holly's rationalization. "You're absolutely right, dear. If this sleet turns to snow, it will be a Christmas card-perfect holiday."

She patted Holly's knee. "Open your birthday present."

Pulling the gift from her jacket pocket, Holly tore off the paper. It was an orange Walkman with headphones. Holly kissed Mom on the cheek, feeling pleased she'd remembered her daughter's favorite color.

Holly spent the afternoon at Beth's house, wrapping presents she'd stored there. She figured her parents needed time alone to talk, so she'd planned in advance to disappear for a few hours.

Christmas Eve night, Dad took them to the Latitude 56 Restaurant. Mom gave up heels and sheer hose for heavy wool pants and sturdy boots.

She'd twisted Holly's hair into a French braid, then braided her own, and had even let Holly try some of her mascara, blusher, and fingernail polish.

After dinner, the sleet did turn to snow, as hoped. By the time they arrived home, snow fell in heavy clumps. Dad built a fire, while Holly and Mom rounded up lights and ornaments.

The smell of pine, wood smoke, and spiced tea, as well as Christmas music coming through her headphones, gave Holly a homey feeling.

But things seemed *too* perfect. She kept waiting for something to go wrong — like she'd wake up to discover it had been only a dream, and Mom was still in California, trimming the soap man's tree.

"Let's open presents!" Mom exclaimed after the room was decorated.

Holly pulled off her headphones, not sure she'd heard Mom correctly. "Now?"

"Sure. You don't believe in Santa Claus anymore, do you?"

Holly shook her head. "Not since Dad's Santa beard fell into the punch bowl when I was seven."

Dad came into the living room carrying a plateful of Mrs. Kanaga's famous brownies.

"We're going to open presents now," Holly told him.

"We can't," he said, setting the brownies on the coffee table. "Santa hasn't come yet."

"Da-ad. I don't believe that stuff anymore."

Dad looked shocked. "But I do!"

Holly and Mom threw pillows at him.

"Okay," he said. "I surrender." He pulled the ancient holiday album from the cabinet, and placed the green record on the turntable. The worn, scratchy recording was tradition at every Mann Christmas.

Familiar notes of "Away in a Manger" filled the room as Dad passed around gifts. Holly leaned back on the couch, watching her parents share their presents for each other. As her mom had predicted, it was a Christmas card-perfect holiday.

"And this one's for Holly Marie," her dad said as he handed her a shoe box-shaped gift.

Her heart raced. Her Tlingit Indian moccasins!

Holly ripped off the paper and flipped open the box. Instead of moccasins, she pulled out a stuffed white polar bear.

Holly forced a smile. How long would her dad keep treating her like a little girl?

She hugged the cuddly bear and thanked Dad anyway, sighing to herself, *it's an* almost *perfect Christmas*.

16

Holly slept late on Christmas day — something she'd never done before. The anticipation of the morning was gone since they'd unwrapped presents the night before.

As she awoke, a sadness crept over her, as though sleeping late on Christmas meant she was letting go of Holly, the little girl, and becoming Holly, the almost-grown-up.

Listening to her parents' voices during the night had made it hard to sleep. Most of the time, all she heard were mumbles, but at least twice an hour, they yelled at each other.

Holly had pulled the pillows over her head and prayed for them to stop.

She'd hoped her parents would include her in their discussions. But they hadn't asked for her opinion when they decided to separate, so why should they ask for her opinion now?

Holly rose, taking a long bath with the mountain flower bath salts Mrs. Kanaga gave her. Then she slipped on a robe and browsed under the Christmas tree for new clothes to wear — black jeans, a UCLA sweatshirt from Mom, and an Alaskan scrimshaw necklace from Dad.

Mrs. Kanaga left directions for reheating the turkey, which had been cooked yesterday. Holly took care of it, then pulled on a jacket and dashed to Beth's.

Snow was still falling. It was a perfect Christmas morning.

The girls exchanged gifts. Holly's gift to Beth was a cookbook of Alaskan recipes for *normal* food, as Beth called it, and Beth's gift to Holly was her hoped-for pair of Tlingit Indian moccasins.

"It was Mom's idea to get them for you," Beth explained. "I got a pair just like them."

At noon, Holly returned home to prepare dinner, but Mom was in the kitchen and had everything finished — just as in years past.

She looked like her old self this morning, too, with hair still wet from the shower, and no makeup.

This was the Mom Holly missed.

As she set the table, Dad joined them. After grace had been said, he began to stare at her. Whenever Dad had something important to say sitting down, he stared instead of paced.

Holly braced herself.

"I have good news," he began.

She held her breath, waiting for the "and bad news," part, but it never came.

He placed his hand over hers. "We're going home."

Holly was confused. "We *are* home."

Her parents exchanged glances. She hated it when they exchanged glances. It made her feel like they were in on something she didn't know about, which is exactly what was happening.

"We're going home to California," Mom exclaimed, sparkling as brightly as the tinsel on the tree. "All of us are going home."

Holly was shocked. Is this what the all-night discussion was about? And Mom won?

Holly turned toward Dad, who was still staring at her. "What about your job?" she asked.

"Tomorrow I'll call my old boss at KLTV. He's been after me to come back for about six months. It shouldn't be a problem."

Holly's insides battled. Half of her burst with excitement at the thought of going back to L.A. But a bigger half of her wanted to stay in Ketchikan. "What about me?"

Mom was still sparkling. "You'll see all your old friends again, and you'll go back to the same school."

Holly ate dinner in silence while Mom and Dad made plans to move. Her prediction was right after all. The perfect part of Christmas had just come crashing to an end.

It'd be nice to see her old friends again, but Beth was her best friend now. Beth was the *best* best friend she'd ever had.

Gary was the closest thing she'd had to a boyfriend in her life, except for Jake Sanger in the third grade, but third-grade boyfriends don't count.

And HJ's.

What about HJ's?

The PTA planned to vote next month on whether or not the snack stand could become a regular part of the cafeteria. And Holly and Beth had already decided what they were going to say if the PTA wanted them to hand over the recipes.

They'd say the recipes had been passed down for generations in the Mann family, and were full of secret ingredients that could not be disclosed.

The mayor had even been invited to visit their school in January to consider arranging for the three partners to set up HJ's during the summer on Front Street, and cater to the tourists.

Holly's dreams were beginning to come true. She couldn't move away now. It would spoil everything.

She tuned back in on her parents' conversation. Now they were deciding which college she would attend. Why did they have to make decisions about her life without asking her?

If only they'd bother to ask, they'd know she wasn't planning to go to college at all. She was going to be an entrepreneur. Heck, she was one already.

When they moved from California, Mom stayed behind for her career. Well, Holly would do the same. Mom should understand completely.

Holly would stay behind in Alaska for *her* career.

17

The next month passed like a dream for Holly. She was there, yet she wasn't. Going through the motions of things she had to do — like go to school — made her feel depressed.

Beth was depressed about her leaving, too, and even Gary acted sad. Alaska was so far away from California, it wasn't likely she'd be dropping in for a weekend visit.

The time for Mom's return trip to L.A. came and went. She stayed behind to plan the move.

The PTA overwhelmingly voted for HJ's to continue as a snack stand in the school cafeteria. The mayor asked the Community Improvement Committee to donate a small building on the waterfront dock, rent-free, for HJ's during the summer. Other school districts requested information on how to open their own snack stand in their school cafeteria.

Holly never dreamed her crazy idea would catch on like this.

After trudging home from the bus stop one January afternoon through weather as dreary as her mood, Holly found Mom perched on top of a ladder, painting the kitchen sunshine yellow in hopes it would help the house sell.

At the sight of her daughter, she descended the ladder. "Ah, I've been looking for an excuse to stop for a cup of tea."

Holly sat at the table, watching Mom prepare the tea. She looked so different on television than she did here in real life, wearing her paint-stained jeans, and an I LOVE ALASKA sweatshirt, with her hair caught up in one of Holly's banana combs.

"Dear," her mom began, carrying cups to the table, "I thought you'd be thrilled about moving back to the lower forty-eight."

Holly chuckled at how fast Mom had picked up Ketchikan lingo.

"But, I can plainly see that *thrilled* is not the right word. You've been moping around like I've asked you to give up your hot rollers and share your room with all your cousins. What's the prob — ?"

Mom tipped back in her chair. "Wait, I know what it is; I just figured it out." She pointed at Holly with both hands. "You're in love with that guy next door."

Holly felt the blood drain from her face. How could her mother know?

"That's it!" Mom clapped her hands, acting as

111

if she'd just won the California lottery.

"I knew it. The first time I saw that gorgeous Brian, I suspected he'd broken a lot of hearts. And my own little Holly has fallen for him."

"Brian?" Holly felt relieved. "I'm not in love with Brian. Brian's in love with . . . Brian."

Holly laughed at her own cleverness — and from the relief of not having her crush on Gary exposed. "Mo-om, get serious," she said, then quickly added, "I have a question," to get Mom off the subject. "When we moved to Alaska, why didn't you move with us?"

Mom sipped her tea, looking disappointed that her brilliant discovery had fizzled. "You know the answer, Holly. My career was blossoming. If I'd disappeared, even for a few months, I'd have been labeled a has-been as far as the industry is concerned."

Holly didn't miss the fact Mom was confiding in her like a girlfriend instead of a daughter. It made her feel good, grown-up even.

"I'd worked so hard just to get a chance to audition," she continued. "Then all the offers started coming at once. Your dad wouldn't hold on until I established myself. He'd dreamed of moving to Alaska even before we were married. When he finally got his chance, one of us had to make a sacrifice, and neither would."

She gave Holly a pained expression. "The separation was not because we don't love each other.

It was simply because we couldn't come to an agreement."

Mom's hand shook as she set her cup on the table. "If only the movie offers would come now, I wouldn't need to do commercials anymore, and I could live here in Alaska in between filming movies."

"Do you think the offers will come?" Holly asked in a hushed voice, as if saying the words any louder might keep them from coming true.

Mom looked as if that were one question she'd rather not answer. "It's so competitive. You have no idea how many hundreds of actresses audition for the same roles I do."

"But you're so good."

"Thank you. Why can't you be a producer?" She laughed. "Most of the other actresses are good, too, and a big part of casting is who you know, what you look like, and simply being in the right place at the right time."

Now was Holly's chance to plead her case. She straightened in her chair, willing herself to look older. "Mom," she began, trying to deepen her voice a notch. "You know all those feelings about your career taking off? That's how I feel about living in Ketchikan. I've got the *best* friends here. HJ's is a big success, and next summer we can really make it a business. If I leave now, I'll have to throw it all away."

"Can't you try another HJ's in Los Angeles?"

"No," Holly answered at once, not even wanting to consider another HJ's without Beth and Gary. "It wouldn't be the same."

She leaned forward, locking eyes with her mother to make her understand. "If you and Dad move, I'm staying here."

Mom was motionless. She held Holly's gaze as if she could read the thoughts written across her daughter's mind. "Holly, you can't stay here."

"I *have* to stay," she blurted, forgetting to keep her voice deep. "This is where — "

Mom held up one hand. "Case closed."

"But," Holly persisted. "If *I* can't stay here, what will make *you* stay?"

"Me? Stay here? Sunshine. Green plants. My rose garden. The smell of clover."

"We have those here in the summer."

"And my work."

Holly didn't have an answer to that one. But she wasn't about to give up. "I've talked to Beth's mom, and she said I could move in with them, and — "

"Absolutely not," Mom said, a shadow darkening her face. "Holly, I lived without my daughter for a whole year, and I will not allow anything else to take you away from me."

"Mo-om, I'm in the sixth grade now, and I — "

"No."

Mom gave Holly her *drop it or else* look. She

moved toward the ladder, adjusted it a few feet to the left, then climbed up to resume painting.

How could Mom treat her like a friend one minute, and a little girl the next? It wasn't fair.

Holly retreated to her room. She couldn't give up now. She'd worked her way through all the apparent dead ends with HJ's, and HJ's had more than worked out.

Flopping onto the bed, her gaze traveled around the familiar room. There were the curtains Mrs. Kanaga had sewn in Holly's favorite shade of orange, and the posters Brian had given her from some of his school plays.

There were pictures clipped from the Ketchikan *Daily News* showing the three partners posing in front of HJ's. There was even an autographed copy of Mrs. Tipton's latest novel.

A bulletin board overflowed with pictures of her and Dad on their Saturday excursions, and pictures of Mom's glamorous publicity photos.

Her whole world was in this room.

Holly closed her eyes, swallowing an urge to cry.

If she could convince the kids of Ketchikan to eat cookies made with liver, she could convince her mom to stay in Alaska.

It was worth a try.

18

Holly waved at the row of tiny windows along the side of the Alaska Airlines jet, wondering if her mom could pick her own daughter's wave from all the other waves coming through the window of the terminal.

She thought she'd feel terrible on the day they took Mom to the airport for her return trip to California, but she didn't feel terrible at all.

As a matter of fact, she couldn't wait to get rid of her mother, so she could begin her newest project.

Her secret plan.

Mom wasn't returning to Los Angeles for good, only to film a commercial in which she'd already been cast, and to scout around for a house for the three of them.

She'd be back in a week to start packing for the move.

After the plane taxied away, Dad took hold of Holly's elbow. "Do you think she suspected any-

116

thing?" He was in on her secret plan. *Everyone* was in on her secret plan — except Mom.

"I think she wondered why we were so happy to see her leave." Holly grinned at her dad. "Are you ready?"

"Let's do it, partner." He double-winked his eyes at her, then steered her toward the nearest exit.

As Dad parked the car in front of their house, Holly scanned the small crowd of people waiting by the gate, making sure everyone was there. It looked as if the Manns were throwing a party.

"She's gone!" Holly cried, stepping from the car. "It's time to begin."

Dad led the group up the stairs, unlocked the door, then stepped back as they all tromped in. There was Beth, Brian, Gary, Mrs. T, and even *Mr.* T, who was home for a change.

Mrs. Kanaga was there with four of her seven sons: Matthew, Mark, Luke, and John. Each of Mrs. Kanaga's kids had Biblical names and glistening black hair.

The group followed Dad into the kitchen. Everyone stared silently at the south wall as if each were unsure of what they were about to do.

Holly never thought Dad would go along with her plan to add a giant atrium onto their house. Not even if she donated all of the $300 she'd earned from HJ's to help pay for the project.

But Dad had gotten excited about her idea of bringing a little California to Alaska, with hopes it would make Mom stay.

He didn't even wince when Luke and John Kanaga demolished the kitchen wall with sledgehammers. As a matter of fact, he and Gary helped them while Brian and Holly moved the table and chairs into the living room.

Beth's mom helped Mrs. Kanaga clear the counters and cover everything else with sheets.

Soon a wide hole gaped in the middle of the south wall. The frosty backyard became part of the kitchen. Beth and Gary helped Dad tack up heavy plastic, which was supposed to keep the cold air out, but it didn't work very well, Holly noticed.

The other workers headed for the Tiptons' house to collect lumber and other supplies Holly's dad had stashed in their backyard so Mom wouldn't get suspicious.

Holly followed Matthew Kanaga down the cement steps to his pickup truck to help him carry tools.

"When did you say you needed this room finished?" he asked, handing her a box of nails.

"In six days," Holly answered.

Today was Sunday. Mom would be back next Saturday. Her sunny California room had to be finished by then, or Mom would never fall for their plan.

Matthew whistled. "What will we do when the temperature drops below zero?"

"Work in our coats," she answered.

"What if it rains?"

"Work in our *rain*coats."

"What if it snows?"

Holly chuckled. "Our hair will turn white."

Matthew whistled again, piling three more boxes into her arms. "You're some kind of girl," he said, winking.

"I know." She winked back. "I'm an entrepreneur."

As she carried boxes up the steps, Holly mulled over her plan. Mom had said that sunshine, green plants, her rose garden, and the smell of clover would make her stay here, and she was about to get all of those.

It was the other request that had Holly worried. Mom's job.

Holly had looked up talent agencies in the Ketchikan phone book, and found one — Tundra Talent. She'd removed Mom's publicity sheet and photos from her own bulletin board and had taken them to the agency.

One of the talent coordinators seemed impressed. If only he would call back and tell her they could find media work for Mom, Holly's plan would be complete. But he hadn't called.

By midnight Sunday, the cement floor in the atrium had been poured, complete with a drainage system so the plants could be watered.

Holly hadn't minded her whole backyard being covered in cement. She never went out there anyway. It wasn't like her backyard in California, where she practically lived in her swimsuit.

The thought of being outside here in a swimsuit made her chill bumps get chill bumps. Knocking a hole in the wall of a house in the middle of January in Alaska was not a sane thing to do.

Holly was glad her dad was just as insane where her mom was concerned as she was.

By midnight on Monday, the new room was framed.

On Tuesday, the hole in the kitchen wall was squared off in the shape of a doorway, and the three glass-paneled walls of the atrium, double-paned for warmth, were set in place.

Wednesday, the two half-walls on each side of the doorway were plastered, and the curved glass roof was attached. The workers gratefully shed their heavy coats and hats.

On Thursday, a narrow redwood deck was installed around the edge of the room, crisscrossing in the middle like a sidewalk through a garden.

The redwood made the room smell like a hamster cage, Holly thought.

After that, the half-walls were painted pale yellow, the same shade Mom had painted the kitchen.

On Friday, a large truck delivered buckets of rich soil. Mark Kanaga helped Dad shovel it smoothly across the cement floor, patting it down under the deck.

Beth and her mom stenciled two huge half-rainbows on each side of the entryway into the kitchen, then painted in the stripes with bright rainbow colors, adding a golden smiling sun on one side.

Friday night arrived much too quickly. There were still a million things to do. Two of the Kanaga boys arranged and planted yellow rosebushes, clover, small trees, and shrubs in the atrium.

They wired huge sunlamps onto the ceiling, installed a sink, then tested the drainage system.

By the time they finished, it was so late, the boys fell asleep on the floor of the living room for the rest of the night.

Holly could not get to sleep at all Friday night. She, along with Beth and Gary, had been up until two o'clock in the morning painting flowers, birds, and insects along the bottom edge of both half-walls, creating a colorful border.

It had seemed like a great idea at first, but it took forever. Holly was sure the wall grew another foot longer each time she finished decorating one part of it.

And now, every time she closed her eyes to sleep, she saw chrysanthemums and cardinals and crickets dancing through her head, laughing at her.

What if all this were a big mistake? What if

Mom wasn't impressed? What if she got mad? What if the California room — as everyone was calling it — kept the house from selling if Mom still insisted on moving?

What if Mom became upset with her for giving the publicity sheet and photos to the talent agency? And why hadn't they called back as they'd promised?

Holly pulled a pillow over her head to block out the attack of the *what ifs*, but one more crept in.

What if — after all she, her dad, and their friends had been through this week — holding boards, sawing, hammering, painting, running after supplies, and cooking for the workers — what if her mom *still* refused to stay?

19

"I have an enigma," Beth drawled, flapping a piece of notebook paper in Holly's face.

Holly had no idea what an enigma was, and she didn't care to ask. "Well, maybe you should see a doctor about it."

Beth laughed. They were in Holly's room after her dad had banished everyone from below so he and Matthew Kanaga could put the finishing touches on the California room.

Holly could tell Dad was nervous about Mom's return, or he never would have asked everyone — including her — to clear out for a while.

"Hol, I'm serious. This has really got me puzzled."

Puzzled was a word Holly knew. "What has?"

She flapped the piece of paper again. "You wrote me a note yesterday during reading, remember?"

Holly nodded. Beth had asked if she could borrow one of Holly's swimsuits to wear to the beach party they planned to stage when Mom arrived.

Mrs. Molesworth had started class, putting an end to conversation, so Holly had ripped a piece of paper from her notebook to scribble an answer.

"So?" Holly still didn't get the puzzled part.

"Here's the note." Beth unfolded the paper. Holly saw her message scrawled across the top.

Beth turned the paper over.

In yellow pencil — the color Holly used when she didn't want anyone reading over her shoulder — was Gary's name, written over and over and over.

Holly heated up like one of the sunlamps in the atrium. She pulled off her sweater, stalling for time.

"So the enigma," Beth continued, "is why my best friend has my little brother's name written all over her paper." She looked at Holly as though she'd just caught her leaving liver out of the cookies. "Do you like him?"

"Of course, I like him," Holly answered a bit too quickly. "I like everybody."

"Come on, you can tell me. I'm your best friend."

She was right. Holly knew she could trust Beth with her deepest darkest secrets — except this one. But she'd been caught with evidence. How could she hide the truth now?

Holly grabbed Beth's collar and pulled her close. "Okay, *friend*, if you tell one soul about this, including your little — *or* big — brother, I'll bake you into a cake. A Beth cake. Got it?"

Beth wriggled away from her. "What's it worth to you?" She grinned an evil grin. "Half your profits from HJ's?"

"What *is* this? Blackmail? From my best friend?" Holly lunged for the incriminating paper, but Beth snatched it away, stuffing it down the front of her shirt. She folded her arms across her chest to further protect the evidence. "I can't wait to see the look on Gary's face," Beth continued. "Or hear what Brian has to say about it."

"You wouldn't."

"What are friends for?"

Holly felt sick. Was Beth joking? Or was she serious? No use taking chances. Thinking fast, Holly headed toward the door.

"Where are you going?" Beth asked.

"To call Ms. Frank."

"Why?"

"I'm going to tell her who accidentally threw up on her front porch last Halloween, rang the doorbell, then ran away."

The color drained from Beth's face. "You swore you'd never tell!" Then she caught on. "Oh, I get it."

Sighing, she pulled the crumpled paper from under her shirt. "Okay, you win." She ripped the paper to shreds. "I'll keep *your* secret if you keep *mine*."

125

"What are friends for?" Holly grinned as she snatched the shredded pieces and stuffed them into her pocket for further safekeeping.

Mrs. Kanaga appeared at the door. "Holly, your dad wants to see you alone before he leaves for the airport to pick up your mom."

Beth grabbed her borrowed swimsuit. "I'd better go home and get ready for Ketchikan's first midwinter beach party."

As Mrs. Kanaga turned to leave, Holly reached for her hand. "Will you still come here every week?"

"If your mom wants me to."

"*I* want you to."

"Then I'll come."

"Did you hear what I just said?" Holly asked. "I'm assuming my secret plan is going to work." She looked to Mrs. Kanaga for reassurance. "Do you think Mom will stay?"

Mrs. Kanaga adjusted Holly's collar. "A mother's heart flies to those she holds most dear, no matter where they are."

Holly wasn't sure if that meant yes or no.

After Mrs. Kanaga said good-bye, Holly straightened her room for the umpteenth time, wanting her mom to see how neat and clean she could keep it without having to be told.

Remembering her dad, she hurried downstairs. The house was empty and quiet for the first time all week.

She wandered into the kitchen. Seeing the atrium opening out from what used to be the solid kitchen wall was still a shock every time she stepped into the room.

Holly was impressed. She hoped Mom would be, too.

"There you are." Dad came flying around the corner, tie askew, hair sticking up, and only half his chin shaved. "It's time to leave for the airport. Can you finish getting things ready while I'm gone?"

Holly swallowed a laugh. "Yes, Dad." She smoothed his hair, straightened his tie, and decided not to tell him about his half-scraggly chin. "Everything will be perfect when you two walk through the door."

Dad was still for a moment, watching her. "Holly Marie, have you considered the possibility that, after all our effort, your secret plan might not work?"

Holly nodded. Of course she had. She'd been obsessed with nothing else all week.

He kissed her cheek. "I don't want you to be disappointed. Your mother is very stubborn — a lot like someone else I know." He double-winked his eyes at her.

She smiled.

"As much as I'd love to stay in Alaska, I can handle moving back to California if it means bringing my family together again." He paused, studying her face. "But I don't have as much to give up here as you do."

"You'd better get going," Holly said, avoiding his eyes. She didn't want him to see her crying like a little girl.

It was obvious her dad thought their secret plan wasn't going to work. He couldn't have hinted any louder for her to start packing for the move.

Holly waited until he flew out the door before giving in to the tears.

Then she switched on the television and the VCR to watch Mom's commercials one more time. Was she doomed to seeing her mother only on TV for the rest of her life?

She wondered what it would be like to watch Mom grow old year after year on television. When Holly had children of her own, would she have to hold them up to the TV screen so they could *see* their grandmother?

She imagined Mom doing denture commercials in her old age with the Chinchilla soap man. They'd hobble away together through a misty cloud, smiling at each other with their brand-new teeth.

Clicking off the television, Holly remembered all she had to do before everyone arrived for the beach party. She still had to prepare the hot dogs and hamburgers.

And she'd better prepare herself, too — for the worst.

20

Music by the Beach Boys blasted from the CD player in the Mann living room. Holly stood in the corner by the kitchen door, her stomach knotted, waiting and waiting and waiting for Mom to arrive.

She laughed at Beth, dancing to the music with John Kanaga, both wearing swimsuits. Beach towels were scattered across the floor, along with a few buckets, shovels, and beach balls.

Everyone — except for Mrs. Kanaga — was dressed in shorts or swimsuits. Mrs. Kanaga wore a muumuu she'd received as a gift from her daughter Hannah, who lived in Hawaii.

It was strange to see snow falling outside the windows while people inside sported summer clothes. Their Alaska-white skin was a dead giveaway that this was a hoax.

Brian Tipton hobbled about with a cane, preparing for his role as an old man in an upcoming school play, *The Godfather*. He limped past Holly in his swim trunks, patterned after the Alaskan flag — blue, with seven gold stars forming the Big Dipper, and one large North Star.

The trunks were as flashy as Brian.

"My child," he gasped in his old-man gravelly voice. "You make me proud. I'll remember you in my will."

Holly playfully shoved him away. It'd been a long time since he'd criticized her and Beth.

He couldn't. They did what they set out to do.

She turned toward the kitchen. Matthew Kanaga was braving harsh weather to barbecue hamburgers outside the kitchen door. He wore a long coat over his swim trunks and tennis shoes, but his legs were bare, and looked a little blue. He kept hopping out the door to check on the burgers, then hopping back inside to get warm.

Mr. and Mrs. Tipton joined in the dancing, along with Brian and Mrs. Kanaga. Holly wished she could enjoy the party, too, but she couldn't relax, not knowing how Mom would react to all of this.

Strolling through the brightly lit California room, Holly wondered how anyone could resist being impressed.

Sunlamps warmed the room, giving it a toasty glow.

Yellow roses flavored the air.

She watched Luke Kanaga spritz water over the lush bushes. It filled the atrium with a wonderful woodsy smell, mingling nicely with scents of honeysuckle, carnations, and jasmine.

Lawn chairs circled the room on the redwood deck. Someone had even set up a croquet game. The wickets were arranged in a creatively random manner, since there wasn't enough room to set them in a straight line.

Holly pivoted in the center of the room where the two narrow walkways intersected. She was proud of the rainbow wall she'd helped design.

Mom now had everything she wanted — right here in Alaska: green plants, sunshine from the lamps as well as the painted sun on the wall, the smell of clover, roses — real and painted — and bugs, too.

Mark Kanaga had even arrived with a borrowed parakeet in a cage. The bird, an obvious fan of the Beach Boys, nodded his head and chirped along with the music.

Everything was perfect — or would have been perfect if Holly had heard back from the Tundra Talent Agency. That was the one rain cloud covering the sun on this California day she'd created.

Wandering back into the kitchen, Holly checked on the T shakes she'd stored earlier in the refrigerator. They'd taste great with burgers and hot dogs. She mixed some California punch, too, to give her guests a choice.

Holly stirred a bowl of S pudding, then arranged a handful of Liver cookies on a plate for dessert.

"Can I help?" Gary asked, leaning over her shoulder. He looked scrawny and pale in his surfer shorts. Holly couldn't look at him without giggling. Of course she probably looked just as funny in her orange bikini.

"No, thank you. Everything's ready. I'm just getting some Lover cookies ready for desser — " Holly stopped as soon as she realized what she'd said.

Her face grew warmer than the oven door.

Gary howled, drawing Beth into the kitchen. "Holly called these *Lover* cookies instead of *Liver* cookies. *Lover cookies!*" He howled some more.

Holly held Beth's gaze until she stared her down. There were a million things Beth could say right now that would ruin Holly's life forever. Would she break her promise?

Beth winked at her, then swatted her brother. "Hush up, you jerk." She lowered her voice as others came in to see what was so hilarious. "Don't give away what the L in L cookies stands for. It's our secret."

She raised her voice to embarrass her brother. "You sound like Brian, laughing over someone's mistake."

That sobered Gary. He clearly didn't want to be compared to his brother.

"Sorry," he whispered to Holly. "Still partners?" he asked.

"Still partners," she agreed.

"Surprise!" The planned yell came from the living room along with the opening notes of "Surfer Girl."

Holly dropped the rest of the Liver cookies and rushed into the living room. There stood Mom, open-mouthed, with Dad right behind her.

She was gawking at the half-dressed people in her living room, and at those lounging on the floor on beach towels, as though a film director had just told her to act surprised and confused at the same time.

Behind her, Dad, wearing his half-shaved face, wriggled out of his overcoat, shirt, and slacks, revealing his swim trunks underneath.

Mom spotted Holly and reached out for a hug. "Dear, what's going on?" she whispered into Holly's ear. "Has everyone gone crazy?"

Turning to look at her husband, she gave a little yelp when she saw he'd also shed his clothes for beachwear.

Dad stepped forward, handing her a gift box, then pulled off the lid, as if he couldn't wait for her to open it.

Mom gingerly lifted a white swimsuit from the box. "For me?"

Dad nodded.

"You want me to wear this *now*?"

"You're the only one here with a tan."

As Mom stared at him, Dad signaled to Holly.

"Mom," she said. "Come get your California punch."

Everyone laughed at the double meaning of Holly's words. She took Mom's hand and counted the five steps to the kitchen door. It seemed like an eternity passed before they got there, even though the small crowd parted to let them through.

"Holly, I don't understand what's going o — " Mom stopped.

Her mouth stayed open in a frozen O.

One foot hung in mid-step as she gaped at what used to be the south wall of the kitchen.

The quiet seemed to last a full minute. Then Mom walked across the kitchen, heels clicking loudly on the tile floor. She stepped into the atrium, taking in her own slice of California.

Stopping in the middle of the deck, she pivoted, as her daughter had done earlier.

Holly held her breath so long she became dizzy. If her mom didn't say something soon, Holly was going to scream.

Suddenly Mom began to cry. She looked so tiny, standing alone in the middle of the deck, tears sliding down her cheeks.

Holly couldn't move. She'd expected a lot of things, but she hadn't expected Mom to cry.

Dad rushed into the atrium, holding Mom while she sobbed. The guests politely turned away.

Holly felt a pain in her heart unlike anything she'd ever felt before. Mom hated it. She hated the California room. She hated what her daughter had done to make her change her mind.

Holly dashed from the kitchen. The silent crowd in the living room parted to let her through. Swinging open the front door, the slap of cold air reminded her she was wearing a swimsuit. Slamming the door, she raced upstairs to her room.

Holly slumped to the floor beside her bed. The adrenaline that had kept her going the last six days seemed to drain from her body, making her weak, unable to replay the scene in her mind of Mom standing in the middle of the California room, crying because of what Holly had done.

Shivering, she pulled a comforter from the foot of her bed and cocooned it about herself. The tears came. It was over. HJ's. Beth and Gary. Her local fame.

Anger toward her mom turned the tears to sobs. Mom's unexpected reaction had humiliated Holly in front of everyone. All their friends' and neighbors' hard work was pointless now. How could she ever face any of them again?

Holly lifted her head to listen. Muffled footsteps hurried up the stairs. She waited, but no one knocked on her door. Voices drifted from her parents' room. What was going on? Were they arguing?

Part of her wanted to be left alone, wanted

everyone in the house to leave, including Mom. And part of her wanted Mrs. Kanaga to come in and hug her while she cried.

Minutes passed. Finally someone tapped on the door. Holly didn't move. The door opened anyway, and her parents stepped inside. Mom, in tear-streaked makeup, still wore her coat and clutched the white swimsuit.

"May we come in?" Dad asked, coming in anyway and sitting in Holly's rocker. Mom followed, perching on the edge of the bed.

"Holly, we need to talk," she said.

Holly gazed at her. "I'm sorry you hate it."

Mom's eyes widened. "Hate it? What? The atrium? No, I love it."

"You do?"

"Yes. And I can't believe all of you built it. Just for me."

"But — ?" Holly knew there had to be more.

"Dear, I've wavered a million times over my decision to stay or leave after I realized how unhappy you were about the move." She slipped off her coat and laid it across the bed. "Do you remember when I told you that the separation happened because your father and I couldn't come to an agreement?"

Holly nodded, sniffling.

"Well, we've come to an agreement."

"I know you have," Holly said. "You told me what it would take for you to stay. And you got

136

all your wishes — except one. Your work is still in California. So," she added, trying to keep her voice from quivering, "we have to go back."

"That was the *old* agreement." Mom glanced at Dad, rolling her eyes. "This is the *new* agreement," she said. "I'm making Ketchikan home base."

"Home base?" Holly was afraid to breathe until she heard the rest of the explanation.

"My agent has agreed to schedule projects for me in clusters, so I can live here, and commute to L.A. doing the work all at once. And, she has a guest home I can use when I'm there, big enough for me to take you along during school breaks."

Mom reached into her pocket and pulled out a business card, handing it to Holly. It said: PLEASE CALL J.B. AT TUNDRA TALENT AGENCY FOR AN INTERVIEW AS SOON AS YOU ARRIVE IN KETCHIKAN.

She ruffled Holly's hair. "And, it looks as though my daughter has been job-hunting for me closer to home."

At last, an answer from Tundra Talent. "Are you mad?" Holly asked.

"Of course not. It might lead to something. Who knows?"

"The important thing," Dad added, "is that we still won't be a *normal* family — together all the time." He studied Holly's face. "Is this an arrangement you can live with?"

137

Holly felt as though the sun had broken through after six straight days of Ketchikan rain. Rising, she sat on the bed. "It's fine. And if I can commute with Mom, that means I can open an L.A. branch of HJ's someday."

"Whoa," Dad groaned. "One change at a time — please!"

Matthew Kanaga tapped on the door frame. "Burgers are done!"

Dad stood and bowed like a waiter. "Lunch is now being served in the California room."

"Come on," Mom said, taking Holly's hand. "Let's go to our first *annual* Alaska beach party." She led them downstairs. There was lots of hugging and kissing, but no one would let Mom eat until she changed into her swimsuit.

Holly sat in a corner of the deck by herself, eating a hamburger, drinking a T shake, and watching the party. For the past week, her whole life had been planned in her head right up to the moment when Mom stepped through the kitchen door and saw the California room.

She hadn't thought about what might happen after that.

Now everything would be the way it was before — only better. She'd still be best friends with Beth, and partners with Gary. She'd see lots more of Mom, and still have Mrs. Kanaga. She might even have a new brother or sister someday.

Holly thought about HJ's.

Maybe it was time to branch out. What about a catering service? Or mail order? Or baby food?

Maybe she should practice right now on the hamburgers Matthew Kanaga was barbecuing. What if she mixed peppermint taffy into the raw meat to make Mint burgers? Or punctured the skin of a hot dog a few times and inserted Life Savers? Would that make it a Candy dog?

Holly grinned at the new ideas tumbling through her mind. The possibilities were endless — now that she was an entrepreneur.

Recipes from Holly's Notebook

Author's note: Holly and Beth could only work on
their recipes when Mrs. T was home, so don't turn
on the oven without an adult around!

Quick Tomato Pie

Crust: 8 whole graham crackers, crumbled (about 2 cups)
      1 t. cinnamon
      6 T. melted lowfat, no-cholesterol margarine
      2 T. light honey

Crush graham crackers into bowl. Add margarine,
cinnamon, and honey. Mix well. Flatten onto bottom
of lightly greased pie pan to form crust. Bake 15
minutes at 350°.

Filling: 2 eggs, beaten   1 t. lemon juice
      12 oz. soft cream cheese   1 ripe tomato, chopped
      1/2 cup honey   (about 1 cup)
                      10 drops red food coloring

Blend eggs, cream cheese, honey, and lemon juice. Pour into
blender. Add tomato and food coloring. Mix well. Pour into
crust. Sprinkle a few graham cracker crumbs on top.
Bake 30 minutes at 350°. Refrigerate until set.

Spinach Pudding

3 oz.-box instant lemon pudding
2 cups cold lowfat milk
1/4 cup frozen spinach, finely chopped
5 drops green food coloring

Pour milk into a blender. Add pudding and food coloring.
Blend well. Sprinkle in spinach. Puree. Pour into 4
dishes. Chill one hour.

Tuna Shake

2 cups (16 oz.) sugar-free lemonade or sugar-free 7-Up
4 to 6 large scoops of lime sherbet
1/4 cup springwater flaked tuna, drained thoroughly

In a blender, combine lemonade and sherbet. Add tuna.
Blend on high until creamy. Pour into large glass and
serve immediately.

Liver Cookies

1/3 cup (5 1/3 T.) lowfat, no-cholesterol margarine
3/4 cup light honey
2 eggs
1 cup unsweetened applesauce
1 t. vanilla
2 T. lowfat milk
3/4 cup granola (cereal)
1 cup whole wheat flour
1 t. baking powder

pinch of baking soda
1 t. cinnamon
1 t. cloves
1/4 cup raisins
1/4 cup chopped pecans
1/4 cup finely chopped raw
chicken livers (or more,
to taste)

Preheat oven to 350°. Put raisins in a cup and cover with hot tap water. In a large bowl, cream together honey and margarine. Add eggs, applesauce, vanilla, and milk. Blend well. Combine dry ingredients. Fold into honey/applesauce mixture. Drain water from raisins, and add along with pecans. Fold in liver. (Do not precook.) Stir well. Let dough stand 5 minutes to thicken. Drop by teaspoonfuls onto ungreased cookie sheets. Bake at 350° for 12 to 15 minutes. Scoop warm cookies onto a plate to cool. Yield: 3 dozen. (For darker liver cookies, add 1/2 square unsweetened chocolate.)

Shipwreck Casserole

4 boneless chicken breasts
3 T. lowfat margarine
½ large onion
½ cup chopped celery
½ cup chopped carrots

¼ t. oregano
¼ t. parsley
1½ cups chicken bouillon
2 T. cornstarch
2 egg yolks
¼ cup grated cheese

Preheat oven to 425°. Place chicken in an 8" x 12" baking dish. Cover tightly with foil and bake for 15 minutes. While chicken is baking, melt margarine in large skillet. Add onion, carrots, and celery. Sprinkle in seasonings. Sauté Add bouillon. Sprinkle in cornstarch and stir until sauce thickens. Remove from heat. Blend in egg yolks. Remove chicken from oven and pour sauce over meat. Sprinkle cheese on top. Bake uncovered five more minutes to melt cheese. Serve immediately.

Broccoli Cola

12 oz. cola (sugar-free, caffeine-free)
2 lemon slices
¼ cup fresh, chopped broccoli

In a blender, combine cola and broccoli pieces. Puree on high. Pour into two glasses, add slices of lemon and ice. Serve.

Avocado Fruitcake

3 T. lowfat, no-cholesterol margarine
1 egg
1 cup honey
1½ cups whole wheat flour
1½ t. baking powder
¼ t. baking soda
1 t nutmeg

1 t. cinnamon
¼ cup raisins
¼ cup pecans
dash of lemon juice
1 small avocado, mashed

Preheat oven to 325.° Blend margarine, egg, and honey together. Combine dry ingredients. Add to honey/egg mixture. Fold in raisins and pecans. In a small bowl, mash avocado with lemon juice. Add to mixture and blend well. Pour into greased loaf pan. Bake at 325° for 45 minutes.

Okra Fudge

2 cups sugar
1/2 cup lowfat milk
1/3 cup Karo syrup
2 squares unsweetened chocolate

2 heaping t. flour
1 t. vanilla
1/4 cup okra, finely chopped
chopped pecans

Combine sugar, milk, syrup, and chocolate in heavy pan. Heat, stirring until well blended. Add flour. Bring to rolling boil. Boil until teaspoonful dropped in cold water forms into chewy ball. Remove from heat and let cool 10 to 15 minutes. Add vanilla, okra, and pecans. Beat until fudge begins to lose its shine. Pour at once onto buttered plate. Cool and cut into squares.

Mrs. Kanaga's Famous Brownies

1 stick butter
2 squares unsweetened chocolate
3 eggs
1 1/2 cups sugar

1 cup white flour
dash salt
1 t. vanilla
1 t. cinnamon
1/4 cup chopped pecans

Preheat oven to 450°. Grease an 8" x 12" baking dish. Melt chocolate and butter over low heat. Add eggs and sugar. Combine flour, salt, and cinnamon. Blend with chocolate mixture. Add vanilla and pecans. Pour into greased pan. Bake 12 to 15 minutes. Yield: about 28 brownie bars.

Icing:

2 cups powdered sugar
1/4 cup milk

1 1/2 squares unsweetened chocolate
1/4 stick butter

Melt chocolate and butter over low heat. Combine sugar and milk. Add to chocolate mixture. Beat until smooth and creamy. Frost brownies.

About the Author

DIAN CURTIS REGAN, author of *The Kissing Contest*, is an avid fan of junk food. She waits patiently for nine out of ten doctors to recommend healthy junk snacks over the four basic food groups. While she waits, she writes books for young readers from her home in Oklahoma.

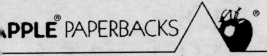

APPLE® PAPERBACKS

Pick an Apple and Polish Off Some Great Reading!

BEST-SELLING APPLE TITLES

☐ MT42975-2	**The Bullies and Me** Harriet Savitz	**$2.75**
☐ MT42709-1	**Christina's Ghost** Betty Ren Wright	**$2.75**
☐ MT41682-0	**Dear Dad, Love Laurie** Susan Beth Pfeffer	**$2.75**
☐ MT43461-6	**The Dollhouse Murders** Betty Ren Wright	**$2.75**
☐ MT42545-5	**Four Month Friend** Susan Clymer	**$2.75**
☐ MT43444-6	**Ghosts Beneath Our Feet** Betty Ren Wright	**$2.75**
☐ MT44351-8	**Help! I'm a Prisoner in the Library** Eth Clifford	**$2.75**
☐ MT43188-9	**The Latchkey Kids** Carol Anshaw	**$2.75**
☐ MT44567-7	**Leah's Song** Eth Clifford	**$2.75**
☐ MT43618-X	**Me and Katie (The Pest)** Ann M. Martin	**$2.75**
☐ MT41529-8	**My Sister, The Creep** Candice F. Ransom	**$2.75**
☐ MT42883-7	**Sixth Grade Can Really Kill You** Barthe DeClements	**$2.75**
☐ MT40409-1	**Sixth Grade Secrets** Louis Sachar	**$2.75**
☐ MT42882-9	**Sixth Grade Sleepover** Eve Bunting	**$2.75**
☐ MT41732-0	**Too Many Murphys** Colleen O'Shaughnessy McKenna	**$2.75**
☐ MT42326-6	**Veronica the Show-Off** Nancy K. Robinson	**$2.75**

THE BABY-SITTERS CLUB®

by Ann M. Martin

Collect Them All!

The seven girls at Stoneybrook Middle School get into all kinds of adventures...with school, boys, and, of course, baby-sitting!

For a complete listing of all the Baby-sitter Club titles write to:
Customer Service at the address below.

Available wherever you buy books...or use this order form.

Scholastic Inc., P.O. Box 7502, 2931 E. McCarty Street, Jefferson City, MO 65102

Please send me the books I have checked above. I am enclosing $ _____
(please add $2.00 to cover shipping and handling). Send check or money order — no cash or C.O.D.s please.

Name _____

Address _____

City _____ State/Zip _____

Please allow four to six weeks for delivery. Offer good in U.S.A. only. Sorry, mail orders are not available to residents of Canada. Prices subject to change.   BSC790

APPLE PAPERBACKS ®

THE GYMNASTS ™

by Elizabeth Levy

Available wherever you buy books, or use this order form.

Scholastic Inc., P.O. Box 7502, 2931 East McCarty Street, Jefferson City, MO 65102

Please send me the books I have checked above. I am enclosing $_____ (please add $2.00 to cover shipping and handling). Send check or money order — no cash or C.O.D.s please.

Name _____

Address _____

City _____ State/Zip _____

Please allow four to six weeks for delivery. Offer good in the U.S. only. Sorry, mail orders are not available to residents of Canada. Prices subject to change.   GYM1090

SLEEPOVER FRIENDS™

by Susan Saunders

Available wherever you buy books...or use this order form.